MAI
ZUCKER̶̶ ̶̶ ̶̶

Abha Sharma is a life coach, a freelance writer and a personality development trainer. She has been an editor and has worked extensively with international industry leaders in online-education. She has a Master's in English literature, with a deep interest in life sciences, and is a qualified university-level educator. Abha has been trained in creative writing and journalism by a leading writer's bureau based in the United Kingdom. She prefers to be identified as a student of life. With an immense faith in the human potential, she believes in unlearning for enhanced learning. As a life coach, it is her raison d'etre to help people find harmony within themselves in order to be successful.

Connect with her at:

LinkedIn: www.linkedin.com/in/abha-sharma-a1774a169/

Twitter: @abha_e

THE MAKING OF THE GREATEST
MARK
ZUCKERBERG

Abha Sharma

Editor: Payal Kumar

RUPA

Published by
Rupa Publications India Pvt. Ltd 2019
7/16, Ansari Road, Daryaganj
New Delhi 110002

Sales Centres:
Allahabad Bengaluru Chennai
Hyderabad Jaipur Kathmandu
Kolkata Mumbai

ISBN: 978-93-5333-640-0

First impression 2019

10 9 8 7 6 5 4 3 2 1

The moral right of the author has been asserted.

Printed at Nutech Print Services, Faridabad

CONTENTS

NOTE FROM THE EDITOR

Many new businesses come up every year globally, but only a small fraction of these succeed. And from among these, there rises only one Jack Ma, or Bill Gates, or Mark Zuckerberg or Jeff Bezos. What are the factors that catapult these entrepreneurs to success?

Discover the true stories of the world's greatest entrepreneurs. These are extraordinary men who challenged conventional wisdom about money and great formal education being the prerequisites for success. What are those qualities that enabled them to create success out of adversity? What inspired them to have the courage to believe in their ideas, to dream big when resources were minimal, and to persevere when things seemed to go wrong? This series explores how these entrepreneurs, who became common household names, not only scripted exemplary success for themselves, but also changed the world forever.

Dr Payal Kumar

MARK ZUCKERBERG

On a windy May afternoon in 2017, as rain poured down on Boston, Massachusetts, a crowd of more than thirty thousand people gathered in the open yard of the oldest University in the USA. The grassy lawns of the famous Tercentenary Theatre were crowded with achievers wearing plastic ponchos or holding umbrellas. The weather, however, could not dampen the enthusiasm of the crowd, as this was the occasion of a lifetime—the graduation ceremony, more commonly known as Commencement Day, at Harvard University.

Among the people waiting to receive their degrees, was an unusual recipient, a smiling young man in a blue suit, who was being conferred with an honorary Harvard degree, twelve years after dropping out of this college. This man had come close to being thrown out of Harvard for creating a prank website, a precursor to one of the largest social media networks in the world today. For that, he had faced trouble not only from the administrative board of the college but from a few student groups as well. A couple of months later, as a nineteen-year-old sophomore student, he had launched a future Internet giant from his dormitory room at this college.

Now, more than a decade later, he was invited to Harvard to receive an honorary degree of Doctor of Laws. He was also the Principal Speaker at the Commencement ceremony from among a bunch of luminaries that included John Williams, Dame Judi Dench and James Earl Jones. As this young man rose to deliver his speech, the crowd cheered madly. This man had transformed the way the world interacted, creating a software sensation that grew into a technology behemoth in record time.

Meet Mark Elliot Zuckerberg, co-founder and Chief Executive Officer of Facebook. He is the man who became the world's youngest self-made billionaire at twenty-three and whose smart business decisions have kept his company at the forefront while his competitors have been forced to see a tough time. The man is worth around 70 billion dollars but wears basic clothes and drives a modest car. At less than thirty-five years of age, he is among the five richest men in the world but has pledged to donate 99 per cent of his shares in Facebook to charity. He owns a company that rules the social media space internationally, but wears a plain grey t-shirt, jeans and sneakers to work and to most of his public appearances. This is the man who has faced unceasing criticism along with accolades, a man who runs one of the biggest companies on the Internet but finds time for charity, fitness, family and even his pet dog.

Childhood

In his Commencement speech at Harvard, Mark Zuckerberg said, 'We all know we don't succeed just by having a good idea or working hard. We succeed by being lucky too. If I had to support my family growing up instead of having time to code, if I didn't know I'd be fine if Facebook didn't work out, I wouldn't be standing here today. If we're honest, we all know how much luck we've had.'[1]

Zuckerberg was certainly fortunate enough to have been born and brought up in a comfortable environment. He was born on 14 May 1984, to Edward Zuckerberg and Karen Kempner, a couple who had met on a blind date set up by friends, and married in 1979. He is the second child among four siblings. He was born in White Plains, New York, where his parents had been living in an apartment. The family soon bought a house and moved to Dobbs Ferry, a calm, suburban village of New York, with a population of around 10,000 at that time. Zuckerberg was brought up here and the family has retained the house since then, pretty much in the same condition.

Mark Zuckerberg's father, Dr Edward Zuckerberg, has never claimed to have done any kind of special parenting, but the inspiration perhaps was indirect. Edward is a practising dentist by profession. He had set up his dental office in Dobbs Ferry, adjacent to his home. However, his inherent passion for machines led him to take an active interest even in the expensive, nascent versions of computers of that time. A technology enthusiast, Edward had bought a ten-thousand-dollar, 'massive' IBM computer, which could do little more than print invoices for his dental office. He later told

Los Angeles Times that it was not about the math, but about the vision. Later, he allowed his son to carry out experiments on his 8-bit Atari 800 personal computer. Zuckerberg, therefore, had a father who was keenly interested in technology.

His mother, Karen Kempner, is a licenced psychiatrist. She worked as the office manager at her husband's dental office when the children were young. She later decided to leave her job at the dental office and to put her degree to use by practising psychiatry. However, she soon gave this up as well feeling she should be home with her children as they were growing up. Edward once told *New York Magazine*, 'She saw those people in the chair, and she didn't want her kids to turn out to be one of them.'[2] She is reported to have returned to practice after the children grew up.

Mark Zuckerberg has three sisters, Donna, Randi and Arielle. All three have successful careers. Donna is an author, a classicist and an editor. Arielle is a venture capitalist and has worked at Google, among other companies. Randi is a successful businesswoman but has also worked at Facebook. In an Instagram post years later in 2017, Zuckerberg had recalled how valuable it was for him to have grown up with his sisters. He wrote, 'I grew up with three sisters and they taught me to learn from smart, strong women. They weren't just my sisters but some of my best friends… They showed me how to compete and still laugh together afterwards… We all are better people because of the strong women in our lives — sisters, mothers and friends.'[3]

It was clear from a very early age that Mark Zuckerberg had an impressive talent for computers. He got his first personal computer, a Quantex 486DX with an Intel 486 processing chip, when he was around 10 years old. He learnt Atari BASIC programming from his father. He had even started writing software at around 12 years of age. Some of his friends, who he said were 'artists', made drawings, and he designed computer games out of them. His parents hired a private computer tutor, David Newman, who came in once a week to teach him. David had later called Zuckerberg a 'prodigy' and said it was difficult to stay ahead of him.

At the young age of 12, Mark Zuckerberg created ZuckNet, an early version of a social media messenger that was used to connect the computers at his father's dental office. ZuckNet was used to communicate between the procedure room and the reception, passing information when a patient arrived. ZuckNet was also used by the family to communicate with each other and also with their father in his dental office. It has been called a 'primitive' version of AOL's Instant Messenger.

Mark Zuckerberg, however, was not a regular computer geek. He was the captain of his school fencing team, too. In addition to that, he earned a diploma in Classics. He is known to have quoted from *The Aeneid*, a Roman epic by Virgil, during a Facebook conference. He knows five languages, Hebrew, Latin, French, Ancient Greek and English. Zuckerberg faces a small handicap, though. He is red-green colourblind. In an interview to journalist Jose Antonio Vargas, he said, 'Blue is the richest colour for me—I can see all of blue.'[4] That is perhaps why Facebook has a predominantly blue theme.

As a child, Zuckerberg grew up in a Reform Jewish family, but he took his time to form an opinion about religion. Reform Judaism is a form of liberal Judaism that is open to progressive influences. Years later, while expressing his liberal views regarding different religions in the world, he mentioned that growing up as a Jew, his parents taught him how important it is to respect other faiths. As is the tradition in the community, Mark Zuckerberg had a Bar Mitzvah when he turned thirteen. This is a Jewish ceremony which celebrates the child's coming of age and symbolizes their inclusion in the community's affairs. Zuckerberg's ceremony has now become famous as the *Star Wars*-themed Bar Mitzvah.

Mark Zuckerberg's early traits of becoming a future entrepreneur can be guessed from his father's recollection of his childhood. When Zuckerberg was declared the Person of the Year in 2010, his father recalled that, as a child, young Mark was 'strong willed and relentless'. The senior Zuckerberg went on to explain, 'For some kids, their questions could be answered with a simple *yes* or *no*. For Mark, if he asked for something, *yes* by itself would work, but *no* required much more. If you were going to say *no* to him, you had better be prepared with a strong argument backed by facts, experiences, logic, reasons. We envisioned him becoming a lawyer one day, with a near 100 per cent success rate of convincing juries.'[5]

Senior Zuckerberg's observations were indicative of the way his son climbed up the ladder of success, with a constant passion for learning, perseverance, determination and remarkable focus that could convince even the sceptics. He knew just the right time to say *no* and the appropriate context to stick to what he believed in, even declining lucrative offers to sell his products, as various events in his life demonstrate.

EDUCATION AND YOUTH

Through his childhood and his teenage years, Mark Zuckerberg showed some remarkable qualities that became the pillars on which he built an extraordinarily successful life for himself, besides changing the world in an unparalleled way. The interesting thing is that these qualities weren't any superhuman traits. Rather, these were simple things, perceptively handled. Be it his fascination with *Star Wars*, or his interest in the Classics, Zuckerberg's childhood and youth inspire one to follow their interests, to explore, to believe in oneself and to have the courage to stand by one's own decisions.

People usually have a stereotypical image of a natural computer genius—a nerd or a geek who is non-athletic, who can spend the entire day bent over a computer, who knows everything about technology but hardly anything about arts, movies or sports. Despite his noticeable talent with software, Mark Zuckerberg defied these clichés. After he moved to an illustrious private school, Phillips Exeter Academy, from his previous school Ardsley High, Zuckerberg continued to pursue the Classics, in addition to maintaining an excellent academic record.

He had an equivalent interest in sports and soon became the captain of his school fencing team. Fencing was one activity that he carried on even after he had launched his company. It was not surprising therefore, that in his Harvard application, a redacted copy of which is now in the public domain, he had mentioned fencing as the activity that 'had the most meaning' to him (not software programming). He wrote, 'Amidst a hectic week of work, fencing has always proven to be the perfect medium; for it is both social and sport, mental and athletic, and controlled yet sometimes disciplined. Whether I am competing against a rival in a USFA tournament or just clashing foils, or sometimes sabres, with a friend, I rarely find myself doing anything more enjoyable than fencing a good bout.'[6]

Many attempts have been made to read between the

lines and discover Mark Zuckerberg's character through these lines. There can be many assumptions, but his liking for one thing stands out here—finding balance in life. He continued to do well in various aspects of his education, even attending the John Hopkins Center for Talented Youth summer camp, which requires students to qualify a talent search test as a condition for being accepted. All the while, he continued to pursue the field he had a natural talent for—writing software. While at high school, he had taken up a graduate course in software development at Mercy College, which was an enhancement of the home-tutoring he had been receiving from David Newman.

In his senior year of high school, Mark Zuckerberg created something that caught the fancy of tech giants like Microsoft and AOL. It was the Synapse Media Player. While listening to music in those days, one could create a simple playlist. Young Mark's idea was to create an intelligent media player that could learn the user's preferences and could recommend songs based on those preferences. Along with his friend Adam D'Angelo, he created the Synapse Media Player. At first, the player was tested by Adam and Mark's friends. The feedback was encouraging. The duo decided not to make it a paid software. Instead, they released it for free under the company name *Intelligent Media Group*. They had the vision that it would ensure greater outreach for the software. They were right.

Synapse received more than one thousand downloads in a few months. It was featured on Slashdot, a website that originally defined itself as 'News for Nerds. Stuff that Matters'.

About the Synapse Media Player, the site said, 'Intuitive, accurate, and finally someone has done it. Check out the website to get one of the available plugins. Another interesting approach to digital music.'[7] Not only this, *PC Magazine* gave it a rating of three out of five. As expected, this led to more downloads.

Soon, Zuckerberg and D'Angelo experienced what could have been a dream for any teenager. They started receiving calls from WinAmp, Windows Media Player, Moodlogic and MusicMatch, as reported later by *The Harvard Crimson*. Then came the giants—Microsoft and America Online. Both the companies showed interest in buying this software. They also offered jobs to young Mark and Adam. It is said that the duo turned down a $950,000 offer. Mark later told the magazine that they didn't take up the employment offers with these companies because one of the organizations wanted them to work for them for three years, but they wanted to go to college. He also mentioned that one of these organizations wanted to 'rip them off'.

So, Mark Zuckerberg declined offers to be employed by leading tech companies, as soon as he had passed high school. What could have been going on in his mind? It was perhaps the vision that he has mentioned numerous times later in his life. Clearly, he had a consistent desire to learn and to create. After graduating from Phillips Exeter Academy in 2002, he applied for admission to Harvard University and was accepted. It was a matter of great happiness and pride for the family to have young Mark join one of the best universities in the world. Zuckerberg's reaction to having been accepted at Harvard is documented in a famous home video shot by his father. The teenager's reaction, as he opened the email, was strikingly composed. While his father could be heard shouting with joy, young Mark just smiled and broke the news of his success. In the video, his confidence appears more prominent than his happiness, as if he knew that it was bound to happen.

Zuckerberg started college in the autumn of 2002. Surprisingly, his major subject was psychology, along with the other course, computer science. It has been widely speculated that his interest in psychology must have helped Zuckerberg in designing and building Facebook. The observations have been both positive and negative. Harvard professor Harry Lewis, who teaches computer science and math at the university, has taught both Bill Gates and Mark Zuckerberg. He recalled that Zuckerberg frequently commuted between the computer science and psychology departments, which were two blocks apart. In an interview to the *Forbes* magazine, he revealed that around the year 2000, the sociology and psychology departments at Harvard were trying to study social networking, but their methods were conventional, like studying snail mail. He observed that his student (Mark) might have been interested in how psychology could intersect with the usage of computer science.

One of Facebook's co-founders, Sean Parker, however, has made public statements about how they both understood the psychological ways in which social networking could affect users, and there could have been ways in which this knowledge was exploited. He commented that he, as well as Zuckerberg, had a conscious understanding of how people's psychology could be used to get them to use social networking sites.

In an interview to *Genius*, Zuckerberg himself acknowledged what people had been speculating. He said that while studying psychology at college, he became interested in the ways in which human beings understand one another through language, emotions and facial expressions. At that time, the Internet, as a growing medium of influence, had facilities for finding information on numerous topics but nothing to connect people with other people. He saw a huge potential in building tools that could enable people to express what was going on in their lives.

In Zuckerberg, therefore, there was thus a combination of great computer programming skill, along with an understanding of the human thought, perhaps a perfect setting for building the largest social networking website in the world.

THE FORMATIVE YEARS

Dormitory suite number H33 at Kirkland House, Harvard, has been called one of the most famous dorm rooms in the world, and for a very good reason. It is the room from where a multibillion-dollar company began, the room where Mark Zuckerberg had launched Facebook. The modest room, however, was witness to a few other software precursors before Facebook became a mighty name.

There are very few people whose college education does not parallel successful entrepreneurship. For Zuckerberg, who became one of the youngest ever billionaires in the world, this difference was meant to be. When he joined Harvard, he had already refused offers for the acquisition of Synapse from industry leaders, had declined dream job offers, and had gained a reputation for computer programming skills. It was only a matter of time till he found ways to manifest his creative thinking.

Zuckerberg's interest in computer programming continuously brought him closer to various ways of utilizing this skill. As a student at Harvard, he started building websites for different teams and clubs. These different tools that he kept himself busy with, played an important role in posing various possibilities to him, including working on the budding idea of a social media over the Internet. Interestingly, thirteen years after leaving Harvard, Zuckerberg revisited his dorm room and made an emotional video that he live-streamed on Facebook. In this video, he recounted how all the different tasks of coding and programming that he had taken up as a student in that room, led him to create the earliest versions of Facebook. In the nostalgia-laden account, he observed how all of those different study tools, pranks and websites had ultimately paved the way to Facebook.

While studying psychology at college, Mark had observed one prominent trait that people had—their need to connect with other people. He also observed that people are interested in knowing what is going on with people who have similar interests. Zuckerberg began to understand that the brain focused on how people spoke, how they conducted themselves and what they wanted to tell about themselves. In this context, he saw a huge gap of social networking in the Internet world. There could be, for instance, people whom one would have met once at college, but there was no way to maintain that connection. These observations were vital in the construction of the different tools that he built before Facebook.

One of the early tools that Zuckerberg designed at Harvard was CourseMatch. Kirkland House, the dorm at Harvard, had a 'beach day', which was an outing for the residents of that hostel. Zuckerberg was wondering which courses to take for the semester, so he decided to stay back and program a study tool instead of going to the beach. First, he downloaded the course catalogue from the university website. Using that information, he built a website where one could enter the courses one was taking and then click to see who else was taking those courses. The idea was that people would be interested in knowing who all were taking similar courses.

The website also displayed the number of people

enrolled for a course and a person could find out which courses his classmates were inclined towards. It also told the users which other courses were likely to be taken up by the people who had taken up a specific course. As the number of clicks on the website increased, Zuckerberg observed that people had a deep interest in understanding what other people were interested in. The website became very popular.

The most famous among the precursors of Facebook, however, is Facemash. In the last week of October 2003, during one midterm weekend, Zuckerberg found himself free and a bit bored. He decided to have some fun by creating a prank website. For three straight days, he coded and came up with a site which he called Facemash. This was meant to be a page that compared Harvard students, not on the basis of their academic achievements, but on the basis of their looks. He sourced the photographs of students from the university's online resources. Two photographs chosen randomly were placed next to each other at a time and the visitor had to select the more attractive of the two. The heading above the photos read: 'Who's hotter? Click to choose.' This was basically a 'hot-or-not' game, rating people on the basis of their attractiveness.

More than the idea of creating a prank, it was the creation of algorithms behind such a site that interested Zuckerberg. At the same time, he was mulling over ways of making such a site more suitable to people whose photographs would be displayed, including things such as opting out of the online directory, and making it more acceptable, without any privacy issues.

While he was debating over these thoughts about controlled settings in his mind, he sent the link for Facemash, in that raw form, to a few friends for their feedback. In that process, someone mailed it to the entire Kirkland House mailing list. Within two hours, it had spread like wildfire and was all over the campus. In only four hours gone, the site had attracted 450 visitors and 22,000 views of the photos posted. Meanwhile, Zuckerberg was in a meeting. When he got to know about Facemash going viral, he rushed back to his room. He tried to start his computer, but found it unresponsive. His roommates' computers too just wouldn't cooperate. The traffic on the site had overwhelmed one of Harvard's network switches. Internet access to the whole of Kirkland House had been cut off.

Zuckerberg managed to bring down Facemash later.

However, by then, the site had received great criticism. The creation of the site included unauthorized use of the students' photos, taken from the university's data sources. Many people strongly objected to their photos being used without their consent. The college administration was flooded with complaints from students. Some groups, such as the Association of Harvard Black Women, severely criticized the site.

Zuckerberg soon found himself in trouble. He was asked to appear before the administrative board and faced the possibility of expulsion from the college. The computer services department charged him of violating copyrights, of breaching security and of violating individual privacy. After looking into the case, the administration took a milder disciplinary action and decided not to expel Zuckerberg.

He later told *The Harvard Crimson* that he had been aware that the idea was a bit in bad taste, but he did not intend to launch it just then. He had been experimenting with a social tool and would have wanted to figure out how people could control their privacy settings like opting out of having their photographs made available. He had not been planning to release this website in the form it was leaked out in. In a November 2003 email to the magazine, he explained that he needed more time to figure out whether such a site was appropriate for release in the Harvard community and that he was not willing to risk insulting anyone.

A lesser-known fallout of the Facemash debacle was the interesting story of Joe Green. Green had helped Zuckerberg come up with Facemash. He too had faced disciplinary action from the college administration. After this trouble, Green's father advised him not to ever get involved in anything that Mark Zuckerberg did. He promised the same to his father. We can imagine what that could have meant for Green. Later, when Zuckerberg offered him Facebook shares, he declined and ended up refusing involvement with a website that became the world leader in social networking. However, Green is currently a well-known entrepreneur.

Despite the debacle, Facemash was a huge learning experience for Zuckerberg. He now had a preview of a grand possibility. He could see how interested people were in using the Internet to expand their social reach. Hence, undeterred, he continued building other social tools.

In the fall semester of 2003, Zuckerberg had to appear for an exam for a paper titled 'The Rome of Augustus'.

The class required students to study around 200 pieces of art. In the exam, the students were supposed to be given two or three art specimens and they had to write an essay describing the significance of those art pieces. Zuckerberg, however, hadn't attended the classes and he hadn't studied the subject, because he had been busy coding and programming for a project that he had in his mind (that later turned out to be Facebook). With just a few days left for the exam, there was no way he could prepare for it. So, he built a website that he called an art study tool. He went to the website of the course and downloaded images of the art pieces that had been covered in the course. On his website, he posted images of the specimens and other students could describe the historical significance and features of that work of art.

The study tool instantly became popular and there were numerous responses. In about an hour, the website was filled with summaries and specific comments about the different images that had been posted. So, it became an online discussion where people were helping other people with study notes. More specifically, it helped Zuckerberg pass the exam.

At this stage, the idea of social networking on the Internet must have been maturing in Zuckerberg's mind. In January 2004, he built yet another tool that he called 'Six Degrees to Harry Lewis'. Harry Lewis, the illustrious professor, has described this in a blog post titled 'My Real Contribution to the Birth of Facebook'. Mark built this site by looking through the archives of *The Harvard Crimson*. He linked together people who were mentioned in the same news story. The idea was that users would type their names and see how many leaps it would take them to connect to Professor Lewis. Lewis was the Dean of the college, so he was at the apex of the connections. Zuckerberg wrote to the professor, asking for his permission to use his name. After looking at the site, Lewis agreed.

All this while, Zuckerberg had been building up the big idea in his mind. All the tools that he had built in the meanwhile, had been taking him closer to his goal, bringing along learning and experience. At the same time, elsewhere in Harvard University, ideas about having an online networking facility were brewing, both in the faculty and in the student community.

STARTING UP

O
ne of the most famous of Mark Zuckerberg's quotations, taken from his Harvard commencement speech is, 'The idea of a single eureka moment is a dangerous lie.'[8] As we have seen, this idea is explicitly illustrated by Zuckerberg's life and activities before he launched a global giant. In his journey from ZuckNet to Facemash, this teenager had a first-hand insight into the vast potential of social networking. More importantly, he had made mistakes but had never ceased to experiment and had never been afraid of making mistakes.

Zuckerberg believed that success comes from the freedom to fail. This profound thought at such a young age, was perhaps the key factor that constantly propelled him to try different things without becoming flustered by failures or by other people's opinions. Right after the Facemash debacle, he had started working on a larger idea. The basic idea was not entirely new, but the available services at that time had shortcomings.

Around this time, there were a few services on the Internet that were based on the idea of social networking. As early as 1997, there was SixDegrees. com, a website where users could list their friends, contacts and family members. The idea was based on the concept that people could connect to a lot more people through the chain of 'friends of friends'. With a hundred employees, and more than a million registered members, the site was quite successful. In 1999 came Napster, a music-based social networking site with peer-to-peer file sharing, where users could share MP3 files with their connections. The company, however, ran into difficulty over copyright infringement issues.

Another pre-Facebook social networking site was Friendster. In the first few months of its launch, around 3 million people had registered themselves on it. The concept was the same: members could share media and other content with their connections. Another notable name is Myspace, that remained the largest social networking site from 2005 to 2009.

At the time that Zuckerberg joined Harvard, the university too had been planning to make a universal online directory where photos and details of students could be uploaded. The proposal was caught up in procedures and somewhat in concerns over privacy issues because all students might not like their details being made visible publicly. The university already had directories of students with a few contact details and photos, which were known as 'face books'. These were mostly hard copies, paper sheets distributed to people. Harvard had created online versions of these directories by 2003, but these had some limitations. Each house had a separate face book and the details were minimal. Most often, the face book allowed only in-house access. There was also an interest in certain searchable features such as the home state or the birthday month, using which a person could be found out.

For quite a long time, people had been feeling the need for a campus-wide directory, or a Harvard face book. For the Harvard Arts and Sciences Computing department, HASCS, this was in fact a priority. In an early December issue of *The Harvard Crimson*, it was reported that the department was moving ahead with the creation of a unified face book, but the time frame of the project remained uncertain. Representatives of the department had begun asking for student suggestions about the design and other factors.

A couple of days later, *The Harvard Crimson* reported that, with the combined efforts of the HASCS and the Undergraduate Council, plans were being made for launching a unified central database for Harvard, a centralized face book. In this context, it mentioned, 'Thanks to a little bit of ingenuity and lot of illicit hacking, a Harvard sophomore was able to obtain a great majority of the campus' photos and compile them on one navigable site.'[9] This reference was to Facemash.

Interestingly, the same news article also predicted, '...it is clear that the technology needed to create a centralized website is readily available; the benefits are many. It is great that HASCS and the council are taking steps to realize this much anticipated community-building resource.'[10]

Zuckerberg's Facemash had clearly made a huge impact and, though it was treated like a mistake, it had shown the way. As a sophomore at the college, Zuckerberg was aware of the developments for a unified face book, or rather the lack of developments. He had reportedly told the newspaper that he could build such a site in a much lesser time than the college was taking. He had been working on similar ideas since he had been experimenting with the different social tools that he had built. Now a concrete idea had started taking shape in his mind.

It was also sometime in late 2003 that Zuckerberg started dating Priscilla Chan, whom he later married. The two had met in the most unconventional way possible, in a waiting line for the bathroom during a fraternity party at the college. The two struck up a conversation and the request for a date came pretty fast from Zuckerberg. He later joked that he thought he should start dating this girl as soon as possible, since he could have been thrown out of the college because of Facemash.

Around the same time, three senior students, Divya Narendra, and twin brothers Cameron Winklevoss and Tyler Winklevoss, heard of Zuckerberg's skill with computer programming. The three had been working on a website which they wanted to call the Harvard Connection. The Winklevoss twins were sport stars at the college and later went on to compete at the 2008 Beijing Olympics. Divya Narendra was an entrepreneur and had originally come up with the idea of building a site connecting the Harvard community. The three had come together and had been working on this idea for around a year. Since the three were not technical people, they had engaged other coders to build the site for them. However, their project had been stalled when their programmer Sanjay G. Mavinkurve left, taking up a job at Google. The three then engaged Victor Gao to code for the site, but he too had to leave because of personal reasons. While leaving, Gao suggested the name of Mark Zuckerberg to them. Zuckerberg's talent with coding had become well-known by then. What was more appealing to Gao was that Zuckerberg could build something that had become instantly popular, that is, Facemash.

The three seniors approached Mark Zuckerberg sometime in late November 2003. They met in the dining hall of Kirkland House and discussed their idea with him. Apparently, Zuckerberg showed enthusiastic interest in the idea. It is believed that he initially agreed to work for the three seniors. They exchanged emails where he appeared to be eager to work on this project and he also communicated that it wouldn't take much time.

In December, there weren't many interactions

between Zuckerberg and the Harvard Connection trio, with Zuckerberg remaining mostly unapproachable, apparently because he was busy with school work. The three were under the impression that Zuckerberg was working on their project. However, in the period from December 2003 to January 2004, Zuckerberg stopped working on the Harvard Connection. Instead, he started building his own project. The Winklevoss twins and Narendra, however, were not aware that Zuckerberg had changed his mind.

Zuckerberg took around two weeks to code for a website that could connect the entire Harvard community. At this time, he had no idea about building up a company or a business. The aim was to create a unified online directory for communication within the university. If the university wasn't going to do it, he wanted to do it himself.

As the prototype of the site started taking shape, four of fellow Harvard students, three of whom were roommates, joined Zuckerberg in building the first basic version of this website. One of them was Eduardo Saverin, an economics student, a person who understood the business side of things. Zuckerberg had known him through Alpha Epsilon Pi, an exclusive Jewish fraternity at Harvard which the two were a part of. Zuckerberg's roommate Dustin Moskovitz soon joined in, learning PHP quickly, driven by the desire to help Zuckerberg work on his project. Andrew McCollum, a computer science student and a classmate of Mark, engaged in discussions about the website that he was building. Soon, Zuckerberg approached him and asked him to do the graphics for the website. Another roommate Chris Hughes, was also roped in. Chris had great communication skills and a good understanding of social communication. The five worked on this project to launch the website known as The Facebook. The purpose initially was to connect the entire Harvard community through one website.

In January 2004, Zuckerberg registered the domain name The Facebook.com at a site called Register.com. He had to pay thirty-five dollars for a registration of one year. Soon, he located a hosting service called Manage.com and rented out space on their servers for eighty-five dollars a month. Since the data of his site was not located on the Harvard network, he was safe from the privacy issues that he had faced earlier with Facemash.

On 4 February 2004, when he was just nineteen

years of age, Zuckerberg and the four other co-founders launched the website known as The Facebook, from the small dormitory room at Harvard. The site was originally located at the domain name The Facebook.com. The membership was exclusively for Harvard people.

The basic blue and white page of The Facebook mentioned that this site was meant to be an online directory that connects people through social networks at colleges and where people could find interesting information about each other. People could sign-in, add a digital photo of themselves and make a profile by answering a few questions such as their major subject, their instant messenger ID and contact details. A person could select their relationship status from a drop-down menu and similarly, select generalized options about their political affiliations.

One could also include one's favourite quotation. A person could find which of their friends were already on the site and could connect with them. One could also see a visualization of one's network. One key feature that was novel to The Facebook at that time was that the user could control who viewed their information. One could limit the viewing to one's class, house or to current students. The site was meant to show people the way they wanted themselves to be seen online. These features, that seem ordinary to the contemporary eye, were quite appealing and interesting at that time.

Zuckerberg signed up as user number four at The Facebook. The first three accounts were for testing out the site. His friends joined soon after, then the invitation was circulated among the immediate dormitory neighbours and then to the rest of Kirkland House. The co-founders had been looking for something around 400 to 500 registrations. The response though, was phenomenal. In the first twenty-four hours, there were around fifteen hundred registrations. In the second week, the number had crossed four thousand. The future behemoth of social media had been born. However, before it could take giant leaps, some serious hurdles appeared in its path.

SOME SERIOUS TROUBLE

The Facebook had started receiving an enthusiastic response within a few days of its launch. However, some serious initial trouble awaited Mark Zuckerberg. Just six days after the launch of The Facebook, the trio of the Harvard Connection, Tyler Winklevoss, Cameron Winklevoss and Divya Narendra accused Mark Zuckerberg of stealing their idea and building The Facebook out of it. They launched a protest with *The Crimson* initially.

The three learnt about the launch of The Facebook through an article in *The Crimson*, the same way that everybody else learnt about it. They expressed their shock and alleged that Zuckerberg had deliberately misled them so that he could steal their idea and launch his site first. They told the newspaper that they had met Zuckerberg two to three times and had exchanged 52 emails about their project. They said that they had reached an oral agreement with Zuckerberg that he would code for their website and had hence discussed the idea and the plan for their website with him. They emphasized that they were under the impression that he was working on their requirement the whole of December 2003 and January 2004. However, he did some initial work for them but then took their idea and started building his own website which he launched as The Facebook in February.

The Winklevoss twins and Narendra further emphasized that Zuckerberg never told them that he was unwilling to work for them or that he could not work for them. They said that he deliberately sat on their misconception so that he could gain time, in order to hold them back while he put his site on the market first. Gao, one of the original coders for Harvard Connection, looked into the work Mark had done for it after the surprise launch of The Facebook. He said that the site appeared to be deliberately under-constructed and the code that Zuckerberg provided them was essentially useless. The fields were there but the registrations did not work. He cited a few other flaws that appeared to have deliberately stalled the development of the site. Cameron Winklevoss alleged that Zuckerberg's site was cloned from their idea, with a similar layout and similar registration questions. He also said that Zuckerberg knew of their plans of opening to other universities, another idea that he had stolen.

Gao also commented that the main idea that Zuckerberg stole was Divya Narendra's plan of bringing something to a specific domain. He said that Narendra had studied other sites like Friendster and other dating services and had come upon the idea of bringing this to the domain of a university.

The Harvard Connection team sent an email to Zuckerberg to immediately shut down The Facebook. Zuckerberg rejected this cease and desist order, denied the allegations and went on with the expansion of his site. He said that none of the code of the Harvard Connection matched that of The Facebook. He said that his involvement had been informal and that he had put less than a day of work on that site and had quit when he saw that the site would not yield any appreciable results. He said that he did not steal any idea from the trio and that his site was very different from the Harvard Connection, as the latter appeared to be mostly a dating site. To the accusations of copying the layout, he responded that there would be an obvious similarity in the questions that any site would ask to build a profile.

He also mentioned that the timeframe of the completion of the seniors' project was not clear and they were still using copyrighted material. Zuckerberg told *The Harvard Crimson*, 'There aren't very many new ideas floating around... At the base, saying that anything that anyone does at this level is new. The Facebook isn't even a very novel idea. It's taken from all these others. It's basically the same thing on a different level. And ours was that we're going to do it on the level of schools.'[11]

Cameron Winklevoss further said that Zuckerberg had simply improved upon their basic idea and creativity to come up with his site. The latter responded by pointing out the exact things that were different — the Harvard Connection did not have a concept of connections, no wink feature and no course matching. Besides, he said that the style and many of the fields were different. Allegations and defence were exchanged hotly, and the newspaper launched an investigation into the matter. It is alleged that when Zuckerberg came to know about the investigation, he tried to hack into the newspaper staff's profiles to get hold of any email communication between them and the Winklevosses and Narendra. In a 2010 article, the investigative magazine, *Business Insider* detailed how Zuckerberg had hacked into email accounts of two journalists of *The Harvard Crimson*, Elisabeth Susan Theodor and Timothy John McGinn. The two were in charge of the newspaper's investigation.

The newspaper had decided not to go further with running a story on the Harvard Connection's allegations, and Zuckerberg had presented his side of the situation to them. However, on following up with Cameron Winklevoss, the journalists had decided to talk to another person referred by them, who wanted to present some more information about Zuckerberg having stolen the idea. Zuckerberg had had a successful meeting with the journalists and had convinced them that the trio's claims were false, but he was unsure of whether they would run a story. Instead of waiting for the morning edition of the newspaper, he successfully hacked into the email accounts of the journalists, using the user data on The Facebook. For doing this, he checked which members at The Facebook identified themselves with *The Harvard Crimson*. Then he figured out whether there were any failed log-in attempts. Using this information, he hacked into the email accounts. The action was probably born out of curiosity rather than any malicious intention. The newspaper later dropped the investigation.

The Harvard Connection trio also approached the administrative board and then the president of the university, Lawrence H. Summers with their complaint. In both the petitions, they were told that this matter did not fall within the scope of the university's rules and was outside its jurisdiction.

Meanwhile, the Winklevoss brothers and Narendra got their site built, and launched it four months later. They however, renamed it from Harvard Connection. com to ConnectU.com. By this time, The Facebook had already become popular. ConnectU received a half-hearted response in an already saturated market. In September 2004, after witnessing the continuous lacklustre response to their site, the trio sued Mark Zuckerberg and five officers of The Facebook at the United States district court for the district of Massachusetts. The suit asked the court to shut down The Facebook and to force Zuckerberg and his team to turn over the profits from the site. The allegations were: 'This is a civil action for breach of contract, misappropriation of trade secrets, breach of fiduciary duty, unjust enrichment, intentional interference with prospective business advantage, breach of duty of good faith and fair dealing, and fraud arising out of Defendant's... unauthorized use of Plaintiff's source code and confidential business plans, and usurpation of business opportunity.'[12]

In response to this, Chris Hughes, who had by now become the official spokesperson for The Facebook, told *The Harvard Crimson* that although they were just breaking even and not making any real profits till then, they had to hire a law firm that specialized in intellectual property rights. That was necessary because the law firm hired by the Winklevosses and Narendra was a national leader in cases pertaining to intellectual property rights. The Facebook also countersued ConnectU in the context of the Social Butterfly, an initiative of the Winklevoss Chang group.

In 2005, as a part of the lawsuit, ConnectU subpoenaed *The Harvard Crimson* to have it reveal all the material that it had related to the two parties. The newspaper refused to comply to the summons because it said that the information was available elsewhere too and giving the information to the parties would compromise the newspaper's independent journalism.

Finally, an agreement was reached between the two parties in February 2008. Facebook (the name had changed by then, as we will see later) paid $65 million. Out of this, $20 million was in cash and the rest in the form of Facebook shares. However, the trio filed a case in May 2011 again, arguing that the value of the shares given to them by Facebook had been misrepresented in 2008. They alleged that the value mentioned by Facebook was much lower than their actual worth. The judge at the US Court of Appeals, who was hearing the case, expressed his scepticism at the situation that the appellants, who were from an affluent background, had received the best education and had all the possible resources, could have been misled on this count. The court ruled against the appeal. The Winklevosses first said that they would appeal in the Supreme Court, but later decided to drop the case and to go with the 2008 judgement.

While these storms had been brewing, The Facebook had been on a phenomenal rise, spreading out of the tiny dormitory room at Harvard, led by the vision of

Mark Zuckerberg. The latter continued with his work, chasing his vision while the Winklevoss brothers and Narendra came out with the accusations and the lawsuits against him.

FROM THE DORM ROOM TO A COMPANY

Despite the Winklevoss brothers and Divya Narendra's complaints and lawsuit against Zuckerberg, the latter continued undeterred, eventually transforming his dormitory project into the world's largest social networking company. Zuckerberg had repeatedly expressed belief in 'connecting the world', a phrase that has become synonymous with his name. Even as a freshman in college, he had been thinking of ways to connect the global community in a more open way. The vision was possibly his best motivation. Remarkably, Zuckerberg was so focused on this vision that the idea of launching or running a company did not appeal to him. Money was also not a driving factor. The exciting possibilities of his social tool were the most propelling factors.

In the first month of The Facebook's launch, more than 50 per cent of the students at Harvard had registered on it. By the end of that month, around three-fourths of the population had signed up. As young Harvard undergraduates, Zuckerberg and his friends had often been having engaging discussions on the possibilities of the Internet and the ways in which these possibilities could be tapped. The Facebook, for them, was one of these projects that showed a lot of potential. The response that their website received made them think on a bigger platform. They had to find the means to tackle the explosion.

The Site and the Team Grow

It was necessary to rent out spaces on servers to handle the increasing traffic of users. Eduardo Saverin, one of the founders, belonged to an affluent Brazilian business family, and pitched in as an early investor. He put in around $10,000 to pay for the servers that ran The Facebook. In return, he got a 30 per cent share. The team knew about Saverin's keen eye for business prospects and he became the chief financial officer and the business manager for The Facebook. While he looked after the financial side of things, Christopher Hughes was the spokesperson for the company. Zuckerberg relied on Chris' excellent communication skills to explain to the world what social networking was and how The Facebook functioned. Chris was also instrumental in suggesting different products and for beta testing the products.

Dustin Moskovitz worked as a key technical person along with Zuckerberg, as the website started growing. Moskovitz had not been a natural programmer, but he worked hard to learn coding and soon became the key person working on the team's plans of expansion. He was in charge of spreading the site to other colleges. Andrew McCollum, a shy, low-key college mate, designed the first graphics for the site. His design of a vaguely-recognizable male face (which was actually an image of Al Pacino), covered in ones and zeroes, had become popular as 'The Facebook man'. Andrew was not really a graphic designer, but Zuckerberg told him that there was no one else to do it and he would not take 'no' for an answer. The five Harvard students kept on working on the site and were excited at the response they were receiving. By the end of the month, they were working on plans of expansion.

Beyond Harvard

On 25 February, The Facebook was launched at Columbia University. The next day, it went live at Yale. Three days later, Stanford too had the service. Interestingly, these universities already had their online social sites, like the Columbia University Community website, CU Community which had a good number of subscribers. Why would Zuckerberg want to launch at these Ivy League colleges when they already had pretty popular networks there? The answer is that it was a risk taken by a confident Zuckerberg. By launching The Facebook at these colleges, he could test how his site stood in comparison to the existing social networking sites. For each college, the team had to work hard to gather the course catalogues, the student email IDs and other details. Zuckerberg mentioned in an interview to *The Harvard Crimson* that it took three hours each to open the website to these colleges.

At this point, Zuckerberg had started mulling over getting advertisements to pay for the cost of running the servers that hosted the website. It was becoming clear by now that his website would expand, exactly in the way that he had desired to connect greater numbers of people. He had already started visualizing that this could go far, maybe beyond colleges, but business or profit was still not the driving factor in his mind.

Zuckerberg's team was also not worried about competition. Around this time, a few other things were also happening on the social networking scene throughout campuses. Harvard saw the launch of FaceNet in mid-March 2004, a site run by the Student Entrepreneurship Council. Aaron J. Greenspan, who launched this site, expressed hope that similar sites could coexist oncampus. FaceNet was an extension of the House SYSTEM website that Greenspan had created a few months ago. At this stage, Zuckerberg's team did not pay any attention to such competition. They were too excited about the potential that their service had, to think of warding off rivalry. FaceNet offered services similar to The Facebook, but in a short time, it became clear that it would not be able to stand up to the latter in terms of popularity. At Columbia, since the CU Community was already reasonably popular, it took The Facebook quite a few months before it could overtake the former. A dating website at Yale university, called YaleStation, had around two-thirds of the undergraduate students registered on it.

Despite these and other similar challenges, Zuckerberg maintained amazing focus on what he wanted. His clarity of thought is perhaps the most important quality that made him grow his project at an exponential rate. The purpose was to connect people with each other and he continuously thought of ways to make this easier and comfortable. Later, as the commencement speaker at Harvard, he had revealed that he had told his friends that one day, somebody would connect the whole world on the Internet. What he did not realize at that time was that the person would be him.

Soon after Stanford, Yale and Columbia, Zuckerberg opened his website to other Ivy League schools, Dartmouth and Cornell, to begin with. The response was extraordinary, with overnight registrations in huge numbers.

The Useful Fun Site

Students found The Facebook easy to use, and it was

more than just a dating website. What added to its appeal was the fact that there were no false identities or profiles with pseudonyms. At its birth at Harvard, only people with a Harvard email address could join. People signed up with their real identities and were in control of what they wanted to tell others. Users had an individual choice about the kind of material or information they wanted to upload. Right from the sprouting of this idea in his mind, Zuckerberg had wanted to connect people in a more real way, wanting them to share more of their real selves, if they could not do so in their real lives. Another immensely important feature of the site was that there wasn't any original content from The Facebook; it was the users who signed up to create their own content. This gave people an unprecedented tool, a power to express themselves without any prerequisites. With the above-mentioned features of The Facebook, Zuckerberg's understanding of psychology was coming to be of use once again.

Zuckerberg had also incorporated a feature from his earlier project CourseMatch. While deciding on the courses for the next semester, students could see which of their friends were taking up a particular course. They could see who all would be there in a class and could take decisions based on that. This feature must have contributed to The Facebook's initial popularity at colleges.

In an interview to *The Harvard Crimson* a few days after the launch of the site, Zuckerberg mentioned that his intention was not to generate revenue out of the site. He added that he had once considered that the website could host resumes which the companies could access for a fee so that they could see the relevant Harvard job applicants. However, he decided against it because he wanted to make The Facebook fun, rather than turning it into a business.

The popularity of Zuckerberg's website at the Ivy League universities saw him receiving emails from all over the country, requesting him to open similar services for other colleges. In March itself, Zuckerberg's old friend and co-creator of Synapse Media Player, Adam D'Angelo also joined him in spreading the website to colleges throughout the country and Canada. At that time, D'Angelo was a student at the California Institute of Technology (Caltech), and programmed for The Facebook from his own dormitory room.

Soon, The Facebook expanded to all Ivy League schools. Moskovitz played a critical role in this process;

with each new school, he had to compile fresh data, such as the courses and the mentions of individuals in the college publications. Hughes, as the public relations officer, also had an immensely important task at hand, to explain to people how the site worked and why it could be useful.

The Initial Competition

Notably, at that time, many students were already using services such as Friendster. The Facebook was a college-specific website. Going by random individual accounts of students documented in college publications, students had mixed initial reactions to The Facebook. *The Chronicle*, the daily online publication of Duke University, documented the reaction of a sophomore student, 'It just has to do with forming a personal web of people,' sophomore Matt Topel said. 'There's a fascination with the whole, "I know somebody who knows somebody who you could potentially meet."' Another account from the publication goes: 'It's a stupid, stupid website, but I am completely addicted,' freshman Emily Bruckner said. 'I just go around and look at all of my friends and see who they're friends with. It's like a contest to see who has the most friends.'[13]

Clearly, Zuckerberg's guess was working. The students found it interesting to join a site that connected them to other students of their college. The reasons were varied, but the basic concept remained the same. Zuckerberg had in mind a scenario where students, some of whom might have been schoolmates, could connect on a common platform.

The number of active users at The Facebook was more than thirty thousand by the end of March 2004. Now, the team was paying $450 dollars a month to Manage.com for using space on five servers. During this growth spurt to various colleges, Zuckerberg and Moskovitz continuously grappled with the problem of increasing the capacity of the servers. Zuckerberg has, on numerous occasions, expressed his gratitude to the dedication with which Moskovitz worked at every new challenge. He has mentioned that Moskovitz's workaholism and commitment to the project had helped scale up the site.

In addition to that, Zuckerberg's old friend, D'Angelo, who was an incredibly talented technical mind and a great programmer, put his own projects on the backburner and devoted most of his time and energy to help with The Facebook. D'Angelo was later featured as one of the 'smartest people in tech' by the prestigious *Fortune* magazine.

The Company Gets Registered

In February itself, less than a month after the launch of the site, Zuckerberg had started receiving offers of investment. While he was not really looking for profit, the business-savvy Saverin, the chief financial officer of the company, moved in the direction of registering the company at Florida. On 13 April 2004, Zuckerberg, Saverin and Moskovitz registered the company TheFacebook. com LLC as a partnership. Saverin and Zuckerberg put in their own money to run the site till then.

Advertisements

A little after that, in late spring, just as Saverin, Zuckerberg and the other friends were juggling with exams and The Facebook, Saverin arranged a meeting with a marketing services company named Y2M. The company specialized in selling advertisements for online college publications. Y2M was impressed by The Facebook's growth. They started placing advertisements for their clients, realizing that The Facebook was a perfect place where college students could be specifically targeted, hence, it would be useful to place ads that appealed to this category of customers. MasterCard was one of the first advertisers on The Facebook. They had placed their first ads with scepticism, but the response had been overwhelming to say the least. Observing the rate at which the site was growing, Y2M offered to invest in The Facebook but decided to wait when Zuckerberg asked them to give the site a valuation they were not convinced about.

Zuckerberg was not really interested in advertisements. His focus was clearly not on making money, but on building a site that could 'change the world'. Therefore, he did not give the advertisers a prominent place on the page. The first ads ran as slim banners on one side of the page. He would not compromise on this when specific requirements were given by the advertisers. He wanted to retain the funspirit of The Facebook, so he refused advertisers such as Mercer Management Consulting and Goldman Sachs, companies that dealt with more serious things like insurance and investment. Famously, for some time, The Facebook mentioned these words above the ad banner: 'We don't like these either, but they pay the bills.'

With a few ads running, expansion to other colleges continued, and with every new introduction, the response was overwhelming. The site had witnessed 100,000 users at more than thirty colleges by May. College publications were continuously looking for an interview with Zuckerberg. The latter, however, enjoyed programming more than making public statements. In his place, the role of communication was taken up by the eloquent Hughes. At the same time, the team was dealing with the full responsibility of completing their college work and for appearing for their exams. While investors and advertisers had started noticing The Facebook's growth, the site was still being run out of Mark Zuckerberg's small dorm room at Harvard. The spring of 2004 saw some substantial developments and as summer approached, a new phase in Zuckerberg's life began.

MOVING TO SILICON VALLEY

As the spring of 2004 passed, Zuckerberg's dorm room project continued to grow at an exponential rate. Around this time, it was still exclusively available for Ivy League colleges. The fairy-tale response that it got at every college, made it clear that The Facebook was going to be a big thing. Running the website from a hostel room, and simultaneously handling a full study schedule was becoming a challenging task for the founders of The Facebook.

Zuckerberg took an important decision at this time. He decided to take a semester off from Harvard, to work fully on his creation. Harvard has this unique adjustability, where students can take a long time off and can come back to complete college. Zuckerberg's decision could be viewed by some as a gamble, a risky bet. Bill Gates had been the famous Harvard dropout billionaire, but Zuckerberg was not emulating anyone. He knew what he was doing. Moreover, he was not planning to drop out of college, not yet. The confidence to take such a decision came, in all probability, from his belief in his idea. Deep inside, Zuckerberg had carried this belief all along, that The Facebook was going to be of importance to the world, something that was worth taking risks for.

At the Facebook House

As the semester ended, Zuckerberg decided to spend the summer more than three thousand miles away, on the west coast of the USA. He rented a ranch house in Palo Alto, California for the summer. The decision was of strategic importance. Palo Alto was a significant part of Silicon Valley, a hub of entrepreneurship, innovation and venture capitalism. The manner in which California attracted entrepreneurs, has often been likened to the California Gold Rush. In the middle of the nineteenth century, when gold was accidentally discovered in the area, California saw a heavy influx of people from all over the country, as well as from different parts of the world. In a similar way, Silicon Valley in the current times has witnessed a rush of innovators and investors looking to make it big in the world of technology. Palo Alto, located in the San Francisco Bay Area, had special appeal for Zuckerberg, since the place had been the cradle of companies like Apple and Google, besides many other notable names.

The house with a pool and a diving board, located at 819 La Jennifer Way, was a single-storeyed large house with open spaces, built in the American architectural style of a ranch. It soon witnessed history. Interestingly, the owner of the house, Thomas Hamilton had no idea of who his tenants were until much later, when The Facebook had regularly started making news. Since then, the house has become a pilgrimage for aspiring entrepreneurs, and for Stanford students, the university being one of the vital entities of California. The house is taken up on rent every summer by young people looking forward to launch startups. The feeling borders on superstition, with people believing that it would be auspicious to launch a startup from the house where Mark Zuckerberg once worked on his site.

Zuckerberg had invited his co-founders to spend the summer in Palo Alto, working on the development of The Facebook. He had also hired a couple of interns from Harvard, who had joined him there, Erik Schultink and Stephen Dawson-Haggerty. Old friend Adam D'Angelo came in for the summer from Caltech. McCollum was supposed to join Electronic Arts for his summer internship. The company was famous for having produced many successful video games. That meant McCollum would be around.

Moskovitz's role in The Facebook had become critical and he was badly needed for the growth of the site. His organized, meticulous efforts were precious to Zuckerberg. However, Moskovitz had secured a summer internship at the computer laboratory at Harvard and he was keen to pursue it. Zuckerberg made great efforts to persuade Moskovitz to join him instead and offered double the payment of the summer job. Finally, Moskovitz too joined the team at Palo Alto.

On the other hand, the company's voice to the public, Hughes, had bagged a summer internship in France. Having already paid for it, he wanted to complete the internship and informed Zuckerberg that he would join when that was over. The one exception was Eduardo Saverin. He stayed on the East Coast and decided to work for the investment firm Lehman Brothers at New

York. He did not think that the gathering at Palo Alto was necessary. Still, being committed to The Facebook, he started figuring out ways of getting more advertising business for it. Saverin had also deposited ten $10,000 of his own money to open a bank account for The Facebook. Thus, with a group of extremely talented individuals, Zuckerberg continued working intensely on the site in that home office.

Alongside this, Zuckerberg, with his keen entrepreneurial mind, had been working to eliminate competition. Sometime before moving to Palo Alto, Zuckerberg had started working on another project in addition to The Facebook. This site was called Wirehog and Andrew McCollum collaborated with Zuckerberg in making this site. Later, they were joined by others too. A month after the launch of The Facebook, in March 2004, Wayne Chang, a student at the University of Massachusetts, had launched a site called i2hub. It had started gaining as much popularity and growth as The Facebook. This was a peer-to-peer file sharing service that made sharing of data between people easier and faster. Zuckerberg saw that i2hub had serious potential and thus, worked on his own Wirehog, which would later be merged as a feature of Facebook.

Sean Parker: The Gamechanger

While plans for the summer were set, something radical happened. The incredible Sean Parker entered the scene and helped change the fortunes of The Facebook.

While walking down a street in Palo Alto one day, Zuckerberg saw Parker moving his stuff into a new temporary residence. Parker drove an expensive car and wore expensive clothes, but he was without money for the time being. For a character as mysterious as Parker, this was nothing new. Zuckerberg was pleasantly surprised to meet Parker once again, the first meeting having been at a dinner in New York around two months before this. The dinner meeting, too, had been arranged in a fairly dramatic way. Parker, the genius, had a keen eye for new technology and an enviable understanding of the business on the Web. He had chanced to see this new site called The Facebook on an acquaintance's computer. Sensing great potential in the site, he had written an email to the students at Harvard who had created this site.

Zuckerberg was clearly impressed with Sean Parker right from the beginning. Parker was the co-founder of Napster, which had become a phenomenon on the

Internet. Zuckerberg was aware that Napster was of prodigious importance in the history of the Internet. In his email, Parker had introduced his Napster connection and had offered to connect Zuckerberg to powerful San Francisco investors. He had also mentioned his links with the higher-ups at other social networking sites, LinkedIn and Tribe. Parker clearly had great connections across the industry. Consequently, the dinner meeting in New York was attended by Zuckerberg, his girlfriend Priscilla Chan, Saverin and Saverin's girlfriend.

Saverin felt uncomfortable with Parker but Zuckerberg was highly impressed. To him, the founder of Napster was a hero. The admiration was mutual, as Parker was impressed with Zuckerberg's vision for The Facebook. He could see that this was not just a college kid wanting to make quick money from a startup, but someone with a vision to change the world of social networking.

Sean Parker is a self-taught genius, an extremely talented technical mind with a complicated personality that continuously led him into trouble. He had started software coding when he was barely seven. At sixteen, he had hacked into military databases and into computer networks of big companies. At nineteen,

Sean Parker had helped Shawn Fanning, who was a year younger, create Napster, a peer-to-peer music file sharing service. Napster was hugely popular but had to face legal trouble over copyright issues with major music companies. Parker had consistently demonstrated his talent with coding and programming and had even been recruited by the Central Intelligence Agency of the United States. He had been earning great money, so his parents agreed with his decision not to go to college for further education. Parker had also been an advisor to Jonathan Abrams, the founder of Friendster.

When Zuckerberg met Parker in Palo Alto, the latter had been facing fresh trouble in relation to his own company, Plaxo. Parker's new brainchild had features like virality, which would later facilitate the growth of social networking sites like LinkedIn and Facebook. Plaxo had reached a user base of 20 million. Parker had influential connections, all of whom were in awe of his talent and incredible genius in understanding technology. He was also known to be a loyal friend and a generous person who would easily help people, besides being a voracious reader and an immensely knowledgeable person. The trouble was his rock star lifestyle. After working relentlessly for days on end, he would disappear for days on end without any prior information. He would often miss appointments and meetings. While in Palo Alto, Parker received communication from his lawyer that he had been thrown out of his own company by the board.

To Zuckerberg though, Parker was an inspiring persona. He invited Parker to move into his rented house and once the latter did so, he became fully involved with The Facebook. Parker was young, but with his rich understanding of finances and the business world, he started advising Zuckerberg about business strategies that would make this site successful. Under his influence, Zuckerberg started treating this work as more than a project. Zuckerberg's well-wishers advised him not to have Parker involved, as a man with such an image would not be good for the company, but Zuckerberg went ahead and engaged Parker. He knew that Parker not only understood the vision of The Facebook, but could help it reach greater heights.

In July of that year, Sean Parker became the first president of The Facebook. While Zuckerberg was more focused on building the technical side of things, Parker was the one who brought mature requirements into the system, such as incorporating the company, getting investments and the crucial understanding of running an Internet business. More importantly, Parker had learnt great lessons from his failure at Plaxo and from the failure Friendster had been facing for a while. He thought he had made a mistake by turning over Plaxo to venture capitalists that eventually led to his ouster from his own company. Along with Zuckerberg, he could see how Friendster was failing at growth; it could not simply scale up. Parker was determined not to let The Facebook get into such troubles. That meant a lot of challenges.

All this while, the small team at the Palo Alto house continued putting in tremendous amounts of hard work. At that time, Facebook was present at 34 colleges. The reopening of colleges after the summer break would mean increased traffic. The team worked day and night. The home office looked like a huge mess, a typical bachelors' accommodation. The team slept on mattresses laid out on the floor and shared rooms. There were empty beer cans, pizza boxes and all sorts of discarded material piled up around the house. Sometimes girlfriends came visiting and stayed over.

The Home Office with a Zipline

Serious work, however, went on in that house, later known as 'The Facebook House'. The boys would work till late in the night, with Zuckerberg staying up even after all the others had slept. He found the peaceful environment conducive to coding. They woke up during the day, and everyone assembled at the dining table which would be covered with computers, modems, cables and other less significant material. This was their workstation. Zuckerberg was almost invariably dressed in a t-shirt and pyjamas or shorts. There was an absurd kind of silence in the house when these youngsters were working. The reason was that even though they were sitting at the same table, they communicated with each other through instant messaging. Moskovitz, who had been looking after the huge responsibility of keeping The Facebook working at all times, sometimes stayed up the entire night. He was also creating the databases for expansion to new schools, for which he took the help of the interns.

The group worked hard, but along with it, they did not forget that they were young college goers. There were wild parties at the house, with Parker, the only person above 21, procuring the hard drinks. Cannabis smoking, known as pot smoking, is legal in California, with a few restrictions. Though it was often a feature at the parties, Zuckerberg disliked it and never touched the drug. The team had some serious fun. In addition, McCollum had installed a zipline over the swimming pool at the property. A person could hold the pulley and zip down from the roof into the water. Zuckerberg had brought his fencing equipment along and swung his sword around quite a bit, perhaps as an accompaniment to his thinking process. There were long sessions of film-watching too, with Tom Cruise being the favourite.

Even at this young age, Zuckerberg the leader, was in charge of the entire situation. He would urge the others to finish work before taking a break. He had maintained the vision that The Facebook was going to be a thing of importance to the world. The college-kid air, though, was harmlessly present around him. On the 'About' page of The Facebook, he defined himself as 'Founder, Master and Commander, Enemy of the State.' Every Facebook page had a tiny line at the bottom: 'A Mark Zuckerberg production'.

As hard work was being put into the site, Zuckerberg

had some doubts about The Facebook becoming a big business. He had seen the challenges Friendster was facing. He had absolute faith in the potential of the idea of The Facebook, but business was something more than that. Parker addressed these doubts aptly, and he began explaining the concept of The Facebook to his friends in Silicon Valley. He also formalized the working of the site by hiring people to look after network management and operations, two key aspects vital for Internet business.

Silicon Valley Begins to Take Note

Parker reached out to investors in Silicon Valley and Zuckerberg was happy with the way the former understood and explained The Facebook to people. Soon, investors and important people started visiting the house. The Facebook was gradually getting the attention of names as big as Google. Two Google employees had walked in to explore the possibility of buying the site and got a negative response. Zuckerberg knew that giants would be on the lookout, and to make it big, he had to keep his company independent. Parker too advised him the same, having had a bitter experience at

Plaxo. Parker also arranged for Steve Venuto to work as The Facebook's lawyer, a move that helped Zuckerberg to formalize a lot of things.

All this while, Zuckerberg, along with McCollum, had continued work on Wirehog. Parker though, was averse to Wirehog, right from the beginning. His experience with Napster made him wary of running a service that could lead to copyright trouble. He feared that problems with Wirehog could prove disastrous for The Facebook. Zuckerberg went ahead with work on it, nevertheless.

By the middle of the summer, even the founders of The Facebook were shocked by the kind of response they got at every new college when they launched. As soon as the service was launched, almost the entire population registered itself. What was more impressive was that 80 per cent of its users returned to the site every day. This kind of response kept Zuckerberg and Moskovitz on their toes. They had to constantly add servers and to work overtime to ensure that the site could keep up with the traffic. The two found out a way to manage this—they deliberately slowed the process of expansion. They launched at a new college and ensured that the traffic could be handled, and new servers added before launching at another college.

With the geeks working day and night, Zuckerberg's site was getting a response of incredible proportions. He started receiving appeals and all sorts of requests from college students all through the United States, literally pleading with him to start the service at their colleges. He did have the vision to make the world a more open place, but there were numerous challenges to be faced before he could achieve that.

SCALING UP

Sometime towards the end of the summer at the Palo Alto house, Zuckerberg and Moskovitz decided that they would not go back to Harvard at least for another semester. That would mean taking off more than a year, but Zuckerberg was working on two websites, The Facebook and Wirehog, and he felt he would not be able to continue doing the same along with a full study schedule at college.

The Need for Funds

As The Facebook continued to grow at a jaw-dropping rate, more money needed to be funnelled in, the main cost being that of arranging new servers and buying new equipment. Till then, the money had been coming from the Florida bank account that had been opened by Saverin. It included the personal money that Saverin had initially put into it. Besides that, the advertisements that Saverin had been gathering brought in some income that was also added to this account. The advertisement revenue, however, was meagre and not at all enough to increase the business. During the summer, colleges too were closed and there weren't many advertisements, the latter being directed mostly at college students. But, before the beginning of the next semester, The Facebook needed to scale up to handle the sudden rush that it would experience once the colleges reopened. It was clear that outside money was an urgent necessity.

One easy way was to get venture capitalists to put in money. That would have been a cakewalk, given the more-than-impressive growth chart of The Facebook. However, Zuckerberg knew that turning over the company to venture capitalists would mean losing control. He was clear in his mind that he wanted to retain control of his creation. The main reason behind this thought was because he knew that his product had a vast potential that needed to be tapped. If his say in the company was reduced, he might not be able to make The Facebook what it could be. Besides,

Sean Parker, now the president of the company, also wanted to keep investors out. He had already had a bitter experience after having been forced to move out of his own company, Plaxo.

Parker had been thinking of ways to reincorporate the company. Zuckerberg too understood the necessity. The limited liability identity (LLC) that Saverin had registered at Florida, had quite a few shortcomings. The company needed a more formal structure so that it could be eligible to get outside investment.

Reincorporating the Company and the Trouble with Saverin

At this point, serious difference started developing between Zuckerberg and Saverin. Saverin had been the original de facto business manager but Zuckerberg was increasingly feeling dissatisfied with his decreased involvement. The team at Palo Alto was working really hard but their efforts did not seem to be matched by Saverin, though Saverin flexed his schedule to talk to advertisers. Saverin also felt that Zuckerberg was not cooperating in adjusting to the advertisers' specific requirements. On the question of increasing the income,

Zuckerberg asserted that they only needed enough to pay for the salaries and the servers. Saverin had always treated this as business and not as a project. He had put in his own money and was worried about getting the returns.

In July, when The Facebook began discussions with investors, Saverin thought he was being slighted. He asserted that he should have control over the business. He started to slow down or halt the process of making money available from the Florida account. Disagreements continued between the two. Saverin put forth his requirements, which according to Zuckerberg were unreasonable. The former wanted more control, but Zuckerberg felt that not only was Saverin asking for too much, he had also not met expectations on the work front.

After Zuckerberg denied signing an operating agreement defining roles for the members as Saverin asked, the latter froze the bank account and refused to release any money. This was the time of scaling up—new equipment and more servers were a critical necessity. Work could not be halted, so Zuckerberg put in his own money that he had earned from his summer jobs and from the odd programming jobs that he had done for different websites. More money was needed, so Zuckerberg's parents pooled in with an amount, as they later mentioned, that was meant for Zuckerberg's college education. In all, the family spent $85,000, so that work could continue at The Facebook.

Meanwhile, Parker along with Steve Venuto, who was the lawyer for The Facebook by this time, continued work on reincorporating the company to formalize its structure. To Parker, more than anything else, it was the intellectual property rights that mattered, for which a safe legal framework was necessary. The previous registration of the company at Florida did not define who owned these and other rights. The IP was the most vital organ of this social networking site and needed to be safeguarded. On 29 July 2004, The Facebook, Inc. was registered at Delaware. It then acquired The Facebook, which was registered at Florida.

With that, the intellectual property rights, too, were secured. Though the bank account was in Saverin's control, the information on the servers, as well as the technology was controlled by Zuckerberg, Moskovitz and Parker. Zuckerberg was the only director with a 51 per cent ownership in the company. Parker and Moskovitz's share was close to 7 per cent and would double with time. Saverin continued to be increasingly frustrated with the team at Palo Alto and he declined to come and join them there. He had numerous phone calls with Zuckerberg but the two did not seem to be getting well along. Finally, Zuckerberg declared that Saverin was no longer an employee and further diluted his stake in the company.

The Facebook had later filed a lawsuit against Saverin, invalidating his stock-purchase agreements. Saverin too filed a lawsuit, alleging that Zuckerberg spent his money, meant for the business, on personal expenses. The lawsuits were finally settled out of court.

The First Big Investment

Meanwhile, Sean Parker had assumed full ownership of his role as president of The Facebook. He made use of his contacts in Silicon Valley to get the first big investment, one that would go down in history as one of the smartest investments ever made. Reid Hoffman, the founder of LinkedIn, was not only a friend of Parker's but had also been close to him during his difficult times after Plaxo. When the two discussed The Facebook, Hoffman was instantly interested, but owing to his own site, LinkedIn, he could not get directly involved with Zuckerberg's site. All the same, he arranged a meeting with an influential investor, leading to a landmark feeding of funds into The Facebook.

The investor was Peter Thiel, co-founder of PayPal, the hugely successful online payment system. Thiel's general feeling about social networking was different from the industry and moreover, he thought highly of Sean Parker. When he met Zuckerberg, along with Parker and Venuto, he was highly impressed, to say the least, by The Facebook's extraordinary growth statistics. Zuckerberg's unpretentious detailing of what The Facebook was, coupled with Parker's clever presentation of the future scope of this site, convinced Thiel that this was an investment worth making. He loaned $500,000 to The Facebook for a 10.2 per cent stake in the company. Thiel joined the board of directors of the company but in a role that didn't involve any of his interference in the day-to-day functioning of the site. In addition, a few other people pitched in with relatively small amounts of money, such as Hoffman's $40,000. The contributions made a finance of $600,000 available to The Facebook. During these negotiations, another key person became interested in the start-up.

This was Matt Cohler, a senior employee at LinkedIn.

During that summer, Zuckerberg had been making up his mind not to return to Harvard. He decided to take a year off from college to work on The Facebook. Moskovitz, whose role had become increasingly crucial, stayed along. McCollum also stayed for a while and continued to work on Wirehog. Chris Hughes joined them towards the end of the summer and even after he decided to go back to Harvard, he continued to function as the official company spokesperson. Zuckerberg relied not only on his communication skills, but also on his opinion of particular features, especially the way the features would be received by young people.

More Challenges

That summer, the number of registered members at The Facebook had gone up to 200,000. Zuckerberg had plans to expand to many more colleges that September. With this, he had two key challenges to manage. One, that the site did not crash because of increased traffic and the other, that the site did not slow down. They had witnessed how Friendster often got stuck in such situations. A similar fate awaited Orkut, even though it was managed by the giant Google. Zuckerberg felt that these sites were failing because they were having problems in growing. Along with Moskovitz, he thought hard and worked hard and managed to avert such embarrassing situations.

The duo also employed a clever method. Instead of just launching at a new college, they waited for people to register in a waiting list. When a student tried to log in from a college where the service was not available, they could join a waiting list and were notified when the service became functional at that college. When the waiting list was around 20 per cent of the student population, the team opened the service and immediately, there was an explosion of registrations.

Moskovitz had, by now, devised a method to add a new college through an automated method, instead of laboriously compiling data from different sources at a college. Extending the service to a new college was a simpler task now. Users could now check out the profiles of people at other colleges too. That led to people spending hours on The Facebook simply checking out other students' profiles. There was also a competitive desire to add more friends to one's profile. A person would spend a lot of time perfecting his or her profile because that would become one's identity. Zuckerberg's understanding about what these young people wanted was getting fruitful.

The Wall and Groups

In September that year, while Zuckerberg faced the lawsuit from ConnectU, without getting flustered, he went ahead with full focus on his work. The Facebook added two new features — the 'Wall' and 'Groups' that increased the usage of the site. The Wall was a space where anyone could write a message for the user. All the connections could see that Wall with the messages. The other feature, Groups, allowed any user to create a group on The Facebook. The group had its own wall-like message board. Both these features became instantly popular. Besides, they gave the users more reasons to stay longer on the site.

At a New Place with the Old Passion

It was fall and Zuckerberg and his crew had to leave the house and to find another place to work in. They rented a house at Los Altos Hills. The environment was the same here, with laptops and other hardware placed all around the house, and not to forget the parties. They also housed servers at this location. Yet, the landlady, Judy Fusco remembers Zuckerberg and his friends as basically good youngsters who were clearly doing something important. She remembers Zuckerberg as a 'kid' with 'baby-blue eyes' and felt that he had something substantial about him. The boys typically worked till late into the night. At this house, which was the headquarters of The Facebook, the membership got to half a million in October. The Thai-born landlady, a Buddhist, recalls 'the three Musketeers', Zuckerberg, Moskovitz and Parker, who had made a mistake that could have proven fatal for The Facebook. The boys left the doors of the headquarters unlocked when they went away for the Thanksgiving holidays. The servers inside were at grave risk and so was the existence of The Facebook. Zuckerberg made an urgent call to the landlady to request her to lock the doors.

The servers were saved in the same way that Zuckerberg's position as the chief of the social network had been secured, thanks to Parker's clever work on providing provisions in the company's legal framework. Having learnt from his previous bitter experiences, Parker ensured another provision that allowed the founders to retain their company laptop and the company email address, even if they ever left the company. The Facebook was now safe from being lost to alien hands.

Wirehog

Alongside this, Zuckerberg's attention was also focused on Wirehog, though Parker still felt that it would be a huge distraction from The Facebook. He launched the service in November. It was an invitation-only service that had been integrated into The Facebook. While it was initially designed to share photos, users could also share music and documents. To Zuckerberg, this seemed fair because in that version of Facebook, a user could put in only one profile photo. Though Wirehog was taken down the next year, it was a precursor to Zuckerberg's futuristic idea of sharing photos on the Internet, a feature that has become integrated with contemporary Facebook.

Meeting Monthly Costs

The social networking site was growing, and thus, more money was needed. Like earlier, Zuckerberg wanted to stay away from loud advertising. Around this time, Paramount Pictures came up with the idea of promoting the premiere of their film *The SpongeBob SquarePants Movie* on The Facebook. Soon, a group of fans of the film formed on the site. Soon after, Apple Computers came up with a pathbreaking idea. They sponsored a group on The Facebook that included fans. In addition, it paid one dollar per month for every new member in the group. The minimum amount was $50,000 a month. It was a win-win situation for both parties: for Zuckerberg, it provided for monthly costs and for Apple, it meant reaching out to more customers through a new and effective medium. 'Flyers' were another way of subtle advertising. For a fee of $100, a person could advertise an event or an activity at their college. In this way, Zuckerberg avoided the in-your-face huge banner ads frequently seen on websites.

The Prank on Sequoia

On 30 November of that year, The Facebook reached a landmark—its one millionth user had joined. There were celebrations and more and more investors from Silicon Valley became interested in getting a piece of this company. During this phase, something happened with a giant among investors, that Zuckerberg is not proud of. Sequoia Capital, the firm that had invested in companies like Google, Apple, Yahoo and Oracle, became interested in The Facebook. Since Zuckerberg and his team did not really want Sequoia's money, on the day of the meeting, they deliberately reached late, and they were not nicely dressed. Zuckerberg delivered a presentation on Wirehog that was meant to be a joke on the investors, besides showing that he and his team were not really interested. Needless to say, the deal was dead, but Zuckerberg later felt apologetic about this incident. Yet, these were just immensely talented twenty-year-olds, trying to keep their product safe from being hijacked.

Need for Funds, but without VCs

The Facebook was now looking for more investors that would suit its requirements. In Zuckerberg's first meeting with *The Washington Post* company CEO Don Graham, the latter was quickly impressed by the business idea. More so, the experienced, fifty-nine-year-old Graham was impressed with Zuckerberg and he could figure out that this twenty-year-old had remarkable clarity on what he was trying to achieve. Graham also left a lasting impression on Zuckerberg, who thought that he wanted to be more like this man. The two got along well with mutual admiration. As the news of *The Washington Post*'s interest in The Facebook broke, calls from other Silicon Valley investors continued.

By February 2005, the site was functional in 370 colleges with 2 million active users, out of which 65 per cent returned to the site every day and 90 per cent came back at least once a week. Such statistics lured investors. They had not imagined this for any social networking site limited to colleges. Other than *The Washington Post*, major venture capitalists and technology firms were actively trying to persuade The Facebook for an investment. Most of this was handled by Parker. Meanwhile, he had arranged for $300,000 loan from the Western Technology Investment, using his links with Maurice Werdegar, a partner at the firm. More money, however, was needed.

In March, Viacom, one of the largest media corporations of the world, offered 75 million dollars to buy The Facebook. They wanted to combine it with their music channel MTV, as their statistics showed that a huge number of MTV viewers were increasingly using this social network. This deal would have made Zuckerberg richer by 35 million dollars, but he rejected the offer outright. He had not created The Facebook to sell it. Zuckerberg continued making improvements to his site.

Zuckerberg's Moral Dilemma

Towards the end of March, *The Washington Post* came up with the offer that they would value the company at 60 million dollars and would invest 6 million dollars for a 10 per cent ownership. While this was better than what the people at The Facebook had hoped for, *The Washington Post* also asked for a board seat. Zuckerberg had a telephone conversation with Graham.

The outcome of the conversation was that the deal was almost final, but without a board seat. This was crucial as any outside control in The Facebook had to be minimized.

However, Zuckerberg had to face a dilemma and, consequently, a test of character before a big investment could be finalized. While the negotiations with *The Washington Post* had been going on, Jim Breyer, Accel Partner's co-managing partner, had a hunch that it was a good time to invest in Internet business. He had asked Kevin Efrusy to look out for Internet businesses that would be great investments. Efrusy got to learn about The Facebook and was immediately impressed, because unlike the other social networking places, The Facebook was clean, much more than a dating site, there was a degree of privacy and people signed up as themselves rather than with fake identities. He made many efforts to connect with The Facebook team and spent around three months trying to get the team interested in a meeting.

When the meeting did take place, Zuckerberg intrigued the Accel people because he spoke very briefly but Breyer could sense a great opportunity and was more than keen to strike this deal. After some hard negotiations by Zuckerberg, Accel Partners offered a deal that shocked everyone. In terms of numbers, the first big investment for Google had endowed the company with a value of 75 million. The Facebook got a valuation of about 98 million and Accel would invest close to 13 million dollars in the company.

Zuckerberg's predicament at this juncture speaks volumes about his personality. He felt torn. The Facebook needed the money, but he felt that he had almost given his word to Graham. After a friend's suggestion, Mark spoke to Graham and, with honesty, told him about the situation. Graham freed him from his moral responsibility and wished him well. Zuckerberg went ahead and sealed the deal with Accel. But he also ensured that Breyer joined the board at The Facebook. His seasoned understanding of the industry would help the company mature. Now, with the veteran Breyer on the board, Matt Cohler, formerly of LinkedIn, and Ezra Callahan for advertising, along with the talented bunch, Zuckerberg's dorm project was slated to become a real company.

THE EVOLUTION OF THE CEO AND THE LEADER

At twenty-one years of age, Mark Zuckerberg had the money and the vision to build a global giant, but a lot of work needed to be done before The Facebook would become a 'real' company. Young Zuckerberg stood for things that were unconventional for Silicon Valley and the way he wanted to build upon his vision baffled many. People were amazed by the way in which this young 'baby-faced' CEO rejected monetary offers of billions of dollars and believed in his vision for his creation. Difficulties were lining up outside his door, but his legendary focus led him to success.

The 'Boy' CEO

Zuckerberg did not have the conventional image of a CEO. He had decided not to go back to complete his formal education at Harvard, an institution that is a fantasy for many people. That was not the only unusual thing about him. Famously, he would work, attend meetings and even meet visitors at his office, wearing shorts and sports t-shirts. He would often be found barefoot or wearing rubber sandals in office. He even appeared for an interview with MarketWatch.com wearing shorts and a red t-shirt with the words: *My Mom Thinks I'm Cool.* Most of the things that remained the same with Zuckerberg as CEO, sent across a powerful message to the world—when the most important thing is to focus on the vision, conventional ideas of appearance do not matter.

The company's first actual office space on Emerson Street in Palo Alto was decorated with multicoloured graffiti art on the walls, in the stairway and even in the washrooms. To the discomfort of visitors, the 'art' contained suggestive images of women and some detailing that could have been offensive. The images were later made more 'presentable'. There wasn't much furniture but for a few pieces, which were DIY furniture that the employees had taken out the time to assemble. Interestingly, David Choe, the artist who had done the graffiti, was paid a small amount of company stock, which is worth millions now. Zuckerberg also insisted on employee residences located close to the office. These were called frat houses or Facebook houses. The environment was that of a hostel dorm and on weekends, one of these houses would be full of people partying. The Facebook people called these the 'push parties', which were unique in that they combined work with fun. Sometimes coding continued during the party, with Zuckerberg and Moskovitz leading the bunch.

There were around twenty employees at The Facebook at that time. Traditional ideas of work schedules didn't apply to this office. People would often work all night and turn up the next day after noon. Zuckerberg and the others would sit on the carpet or even on the floor and get engrossed with work. The company, actually a room called the 'dorm room' had, besides the other hardware, an Xbox. Despite the casual appearance of this office space, Zuckerberg led a group of intensely focused people who worked very hard. The site had reached a landmark of 5 million users by October 2005. To keep the technology up to the mark, the company spent more than 4 million dollars on their data centres. There were glaring errors as well, but along with Zuckerberg, D'Angelo and Moskovitz worked relentlessly to brace up with every new technological challenge.

One big task that Zuckerberg faced was recruiting new people to grow the company. There was no shortage of talent in Silicon Valley, but as expected, people were sceptical about working for a twenty-one-year-old college dropout. Sean Parker's reputation as a spoilt, party-loving bad guy also came in the way. One of Zuckerberg's business cards read: 'I'm CEO...bitch!' Thankfully, at business meetings, he shared a different business card that simply read 'CEO'. In the business world, social networking itself was not yet seen as a business and was treated more like a passing trend.

Robin Reed, who specialized in recruiting for start-up companies, was hired. A practising Buddhist, Reed not only worked hard to find new people for key positions, but also taught Mark some meditation, that the CEO tried and found useful. Reed's contribution is greatly valued but it did not begin without some frustration. Zuckerberg had a clear bias towards young people as he thought they could be better programmers. College dropouts were preferred. Traditional 'corporate' people did not fit into The Facebook's culture, which was all about creativity and experimenting. The Facebook wanted people who could understand the 'hacker way' of doing things and did not only follow textbook corporate affairs. One interesting hire was Charlie Cheever, an employee of Microsoft who, as Zuckerberg found out, had faced disciplinary action at Harvard because he had downloaded information about students and had built a program using which one could find out who all were roommates and similar information. Zuckerberg found that impressive. A few older people joined the company over a period of time, but the programmers were mostly very young people.

As fresh recruits joined the company, some confusion ruled the air. As an individual, Zuckerberg was not very communicative and this confused many of his employees. He didn't think that it was necessary to communicate what he was doing about the business and it made people insecure about where the company was going. A conventional CEO is not supposed to make himself available easily for business meetings, but Zuckerberg casually met other important people from the industry, sending out the wrong signals that he might be talking to investors or buyers.

After getting some hints from the older bunch, Zuckerberg started working towards making himself a more apparent leader. He hired an executive coach. He also started studying other leaders that he liked. For instance, he shadowed *The Washington Post* CEO Don Graham for a few days to observe his style of functioning. After this, he started organizing 'all hands meets' with all his employees. He worked on himself and in some time, he appeared to be conducting himself more like a leader. With the Chief Operating Officer Owen Van Natta looking after the business part, Zuckerberg focused more on the product.

The Facebook Becomes Facebook

Sean Parker, who was instrumental in ensuring that Zuckerberg always remained the head of the company, had also been insisting that the company should drop the 'The' from its name. The organization became Facebook.com after purchasing the Facebook. com domain name from AboutFace for $200,000. The official name, Facebook.com, came into effect from 20 September 2005.

Parker Has to Leave

As much as Sean Parker had contributed to the initial growth of the company, and in securing Zuckerberg's position as the chief, his personal ways remained unchanged. In August of that year, he had rented a house for a vacation on a beach in North Carolina. In one of the parties at that house, a lot of people unknown to Parker had joined in, who had been invited by the kiteboarding instructors. Two days after that, police found cocaine in the house and Parker was arrested. Because of ambiguity about the lack of evidence against him, there was no formal criminal charge against him and he was immediately released. However, the episode did not go down well with the board members of Facebook, who felt that if the company president's name had been associated somehow with drugs, it would bring a bad name to the organization. Zuckerberg reluctantly agreed, and Parker quit Facebook. While leaving, Parker did another thing that solidified Zuckerberg's position—he assigned his board seat to him. That meant that Zuckerberg controlled three out of the five board seats, giving him complete control. However, even after the exit, Zuckerberg continued to discuss things with Parker.

The Strife about Advertising

Ever since Zuckerberg had started with Facebook, he had been against advertisements that diverted the user's attention from the Facebook experience. This led to a lot of internal tension between the CEO and the smart, experienced executives Facebook had hired from Silicon Valley. They were used to looking at start-ups as businesses, not as utilities. Zuckerberg repeatedly called Facebook a 'utility'. The bland word further confused everyone. What he meant was that his vision was not to make Facebook a 'cool' site, but to make it useful for anyone who registered on it. His belief was that if people found it useful, membership and usage would increase, while cool things had a limited life span. While the veterans wanted to make the business profitable, Zuckerberg insisted that they focus on creating a more useful product first. Revenue mattered to him only to the extent that it could manage the running costs. Thus, he outrightly rejected the standard practices of Internet advertising. He did not even accept a one-million-dollar-offer from Sprite that asked for the Facebook page to become green for just a day. The soft drink company was launching its new packaging. So, sponsored groups and targeted advertising through Facebook contacts remained the most prominent, besides the deal with Microsoft that ensured a minimum payment. Zuckerberg maintained that the advertisements should be useful for the viewer. He told his advertisement sales head Mike Murphy, 'I don't hate all advertising. I just hate advertising that stinks.'[14]

New Features and the Incredible Growth of Facebook

By the autumn of 2005, 85 per cent of the college students in the United States were Facebook members. Zuckerberg had always wanted to include the whole world in his vision. For a while, the next step was launching at high schools. That appeared to be a challenge because Facebook had an exclusive college air about it. Besides, Zuckerberg was proud of the fact that only people with a valid college email address could join, ensuring that people joined with real identities.

This also meant a protection of the users' information because their information would only be shared with people they had added as friends. High school students did not have any official mail addresses. So, Facebook found a way out—college students could invite their friends in high school to join. The high school version was launched in September but, for some time, was kept separate from the college version. The two were merged in February 2006 and by April 2006, a million high school students had joined. Meanwhile, in October, Facebook had also launched at universities in the United Kingdom.

Zuckerberg, while working on Wirehog, had always believed that sharing photos would be useful and interesting for Facebook members. A talented team of programmers, along with Scott Marlette, a 'programming genius', worked on the idea of building a photos application, on top of Facebook, in a way uniting Wirehog with Facebook. The team designed a feature that would ensure that the photos loaded quickly on to the site. In late October, Facebook launched the 'photos' feature along with the feature of 'tagging'. These were instant hits and resulted in an incredible increase in usage. For Zuckerberg, this meant that people were using more of their real identity to interact, just as he had wanted. The experienced Jeff Rothschild, co-founder of Veritas and one of the great talents at Facebook, helped manage the increased load on the servers.

After high school, Zuckerberg thought the next logical step would be to expand to workplaces. In April 2006, Facebook was launched for corporate employees, and it was called work networks. Unlike the high school project, this time the response was discouraging. Facebook did not see a substantial increase in registration and usage. People in workplaces perhaps did not find much appeal in this service. Zuckerberg's team were disappointed and even sceptical about the universal appeal of Facebook. He, on the other hand, maintained his cool and did not let the failure stop him from thinking big.

Facebook Wasn't Created for Being Sold Off

Facebook was growing, and so was Silicon Valley's interest in buying it. Had it not been for Zuckerberg's determination, Facebook would have been acquired by at least one of the many big names that came to it.

One after the other, incredible offers came to him, but Zuckerberg maintained that he did not want to sell the company, not even when money was badly needed. He had the firm conviction that Facebook was meant to be a platform for the future and selling it would be like killing an infant.

One of the most stressful times in Zuckerberg's life came when Yahoo came up with an offer to buy Facebook for one billion dollars. Facebook employees were elated, as it could mean that many of them would become millionaires. Facebook's board of directors, except Mark, felt this was an offer that could not be resisted. Zuckerberg was in a dilemma. He clearly did not want to sell his baby, but some time ago, when enough funds were not being raised, under pressure from the board and advisors, he had agreed that if someone came up with an offer of one billion, he would take it. Now, Yahoo was standing at the door with that figure.

While the negotiations with Yahoo were going on, Zuckerberg often spent sleepless nights. He would drive around aimlessly or walk around in deep thought. He knew that this offer would mean a lot to the people working for him. However, he had the belief that if he could carry on with the development of Facebook the way he had envisioned, it would be worth a lot more than one billion dollars. He also had in mind an idea called the News Feed. He strongly believed that if this feature succeeded, Facebook would be worth a lot more than a few billion dollars. His original partner, Dustin Moskovitz as well as Sean Parker, shared his belief. To the board, and to the older members of the company, not accepting the offer seemed crazy. Author David Kirkpatrick has documented the dialogue between Matt Cohler and Zuckerberg that says it all:

Cohler said, 'Mark, I'm open to having my mind changed. Explain it to me.'

Zuckerberg answered, 'I can't really explain it. I just know.'[15]

While Mark's mind was caught up in the predicament, things automatically became easy for him, as if the universe had conspired to help him follow his dream. In July, Yahoo's stock came down by 22 per cent in a single day. Consequently, Yahoo reduced its offer from one billion to 850 million dollars. Facebook of course said no, and Zuckerberg was relieved of the stress of making a bad decision for his employees.

Facebook's competitor, MySpace, had also

approached it for an acquisition. Again, Zuckerberg had dismissed the offer, citing the reason that a media company would not understand the technology Facebook stood for. MySpace itself was acquired by NewsCorp shortly after that.

By February, Facebook had become the seventh most-trafficked site on the Internet, and despite its revenue of 20 million dollars, it did not have a profit. With the increased usage, more money was needed. Zuckerberg's team of executives often became frustrated in understanding what Mark was trying to do by not selling and by not even accepting lucrative advertisement deals. To tide over the crisis meanwhile, more investments of around 27 million dollars were arranged. After Yahoo's one-billion-dollar bid, Facebook was constantly flooded with offers for a buyout.

Another bait for Facebook came in the form of an offer from MTV Networks, although had been spurned earlier. This time, the company came back again with an offer of 1.5 billion dollars for a buyout. Zuckerberg was not even interested and by this time, his team also had made peace with the idea that he is not going to sell the company. His answer to MTV's CEO Michael Wolf is legendary. He said, 'I think it is worth a lot more...

I don't really need that kind of money. And anyway, I may never have an idea as good as this one.'[16] At that time, he was living in a one-bedroom apartment with barely any furniture and he had taken Wolf to his apartment before the conversation. Mark also had in his mind that Google could eventually become what it is by not selling itself early.

On the personal front, in the summer of 2006, Mark was reunited with his Harvard girlfriend Priscilla Chan, who had, by now, graduated from Harvard. She put a condition that they would have some minimum amount of quality time outside of his workplace, Facebook. Many years later, in his commencement speech, Mark thanked Harvard for being the place where the two had met.

Zuckerberg was by now the leader in charge. He knew how to assert himself and more importantly, he knew exactly when to say no. He had been proven right in following his hunch. Along with the success of Facebook, came the celebrity status. He was now a public figure. Eventually, Zuckerberg's vision would come true and change the history of the Internet forever. But the path to that was rocky and full of hurdles.

THE TREK TO THE TOP

Mark Zuckerberg has time and again expressed the idea that success comes from the freedom to make mistakes. Even as a young boy, he had never been afraid of trying out new things—he had created Facemash. He had never curbed his creativity—he created Synapse. He had always stood like a rock against the tides of scepticism—he refused to sell out even for the best possible offers. He knew he could make mistakes, but he never let that fear stall his progress. What is most impressive is his readiness to accept his mistakes, learn from them and to have the heart to apologize to the world for them.

The Momentary Villain

Since 2005, Zuckerberg and his core team had been brainstorming about a feature they called the News

Feed. It was supposed to be a personalized newspaper on a person's Facebook page. The idea was to bring to the person the news that mattered to him the most—things that were going on with his friends, rather than news from far corners of the world that the person could not really associate with. To bring that to each person's page, the team worked hard for many months as it was a huge technological challenge—Facebook had to customize each of its 9.4 million user pages, so that it could show the activities related to the person's friends. To Zuckerberg, this was not just a feature, it was an evolution for Facebook. News Feed was launched on 5 September 2006 with a note from Ruchi Sanghvi, the News Feed product manager. The note explained that it would keep the user updated about the activities in their social circles and the mini feed would tell them about the changes in a person's profile.

The immediate reaction to the News Feed was a shocker—people hated it. It was a crisis for Facebook. The company started receiving hate messages. The service gave the users the feeling of being stalked and of stalking. Too much information was being sent to a user's friends, and the user was in greater discomfort if they had collected too many 'friends' but did not want to share any updates with all of them. About five hundred protest groups were quickly formed on Facebook itself. A group called 'Students Against Facebook News Feed' had gathered about 700,000 people in three days. Ruchi was called the devil. The number was worrisome— 10 per cent of Facebook users were actively protesting. Facebook's office was surrounded by media crews and the protestors planned an in-person demonstration. The company had to hire a security agency to escort their employees in and out of the office.

In this situation, Zuckerberg took the lead and wrote a blog with the headline 'Calm down. Breathe. We hear you.' He calmly tried to explain that News Feed simply shared only the stuff that would have been available on a profile even otherwise. But the protests continued. Zuckerberg and his team worked incessantly for two days and brought in privacy features that gave users greater control over sharing information. He wrote another blog post on Facebook that speaks a lot about his inherent personality—he apologized. He started with, 'We really messed this one up... We didn't build in the proper privacy controls right away. This was a big mistake on our part and I'm sorry for it.' The protests were then cancelled.

It is noteworthy that though the groups were sending hate messages and were writing all sorts of bad things about Facebook, Zuckerberg did not think of blocking or turning off those groups. He believed that it would be against journalistic integrity to block the messages from showing up in people's News Feeds. His idea of openness was more important to him.

At the same time, Zuckerberg could see the irony of the situation. People were protesting against News Feed, but it was the same service that made it possible to form protest groups so quickly. That was the immense power in the hands of the people and it showed that News Feed had actually been successful. The same feature would go on to become one of the most popular features of this social network.

The World Joins Facebook

Even though this was a scary experience for Facebook, Zuckerberg was not even slightly agitated. He knew that this feature would work; perhaps the timing had been wrong. He went ahead with his long-standing desire to make Facebook open to all, and just two weeks after the News Feed episode, made Facebook open to the world. The only criterion was for a person to be thirteen years or older. The response was heartwarming. Around 50,000 people were joining in a day. By December, Facebook had 12 million active users.

Zuckerberg now started receiving praise for his leadership and he was just twenty-two years old at that time. Gradually, the News Feed became popular and, coupled with open registration, took Facebook a long way. That was the time for Zuckerberg to substantiate his long-standing dream of turning Facebook into a platform. This was going to be a revolutionary idea, like Bill Gates' Microsoft platform on which people could build applications. Only, these were going to be social applications in sync with the spirit of Facebook.

A New Revolution

On 24 May 2007, around 750 people from the media and from software companies had gathered at San Francisco for an event called f8. The only thing these people knew was that Facebook was going to make a big announcement that day. They had no idea of the incredible amount of work that had been put in by Zuckerberg and his team for months, to make

Facebook a platform. As Zuckerberg began his address to the gathering, the slides on the screen did not seem to match his presentation and his speech went out of sync with the visuals. He paused and diffused the discomfort in the air by making a light comment. Soon, he restarted in coordination with the visuals and it turned out to be a smooth presentation. It did not matter if Zuckerberg was generally perceived as awkward, socially. That tag had changed and so had the Internet. Making Facebook a platform meant that anyone in the world could build an application on Facebook.

What was more striking was that Facebook went to a great length to ensure that while it invited people to build upon its platform, Facebook itself did not have an unfair advantage. Zuckerberg wanted it to be a level playing field and had even removed some of the features from the photos application and the courses application. The message was clear—Facebook would have no advantage over the outside developers. This extent of freedom, given to the developers, was extraordinary. The world was excited. Only a few people knew that the idea of making Facebook a platform had led to a lot of internal argument. There was concern about a simple logistical aspect—if outside developers were allowed to add applications for free and were even allowed to have advertisements in them, they would be making money, but Facebook would be getting nothing out of it.

The concern seemed valid, but Zuckerberg stuck to his decision. As the events unfolded, he was proved right. His reasoning was that inviting developers would increase the traffic on the site. Besides, Facebook could always reserve a slot for advertisements on the application. Another related event was this direct. Sometime ago, the most popular social network at that time, MySpace, had declared that it would not allow any third-party applications on its site. This is what differentiated it from Zuckerberg's vision—he was passionate about technology and the former running a media business.

Zuckerberg's unconventional vision was proved correct once again. The response to the platform was phenomenal. Facebook people worked overtime to install numerous new servers to handle the rush. Within months, 25,000 applications were running on Facebook. The number of users skyrocketed from 24 million to 70 million within a year. Soon, Facebook was way ahead of MySpace. The kind of applications, though, turned out to be a little unsatisfactory for Zuckerberg at first. He was hoping for substantial things, but games turned out to be the most popular of applications on Facebook. Notable among these is Lexulous, a word game developed by the Indian brothers Jayant and Rajat Agarwalla. The game was initially launched as Scrabulous, a copy of Scrabble, but after some legal issues it came in its new avatar. *PC World* magazine had rated Scrabulous at number 15 among the hundred best products of 2008. The game had caught Mark's attention when it made his grandparents join Facebook. Some serious things were also being built on the platform. Joe Green, Mark's Facemash aide, and Sean Parker designed Causes, that was meant to help non-profit organizations raise money, and Zuckerberg really liked this one.

The platform transformed a lot of things and once again, as Zuckerberg had visualized, Facebook became a hub for a new kind of social activity. The companies building applications for Facebook had become so successful that, by 2009, their collective revenue was almost the same as that of Facebook itself, with some games having a monthly revenue of as much as 3 million dollars.

A problem soon surfaced. Facebook saw an influx of inappropriate applications as well. In the second f8 the next year, Zuckerberg announced several measures that Facebook would incorporate to rate applications and to remove inappropriate ones. f8 had come from the words 'Facebook' and the '8-hour hackathons' that would become a regular feature of the Facebook culture. A hack marathon or a hackathon was an intensive all-night session where programmers competed to create new and innovative ideas. The coding took place there and then, but the only rule was that the coders could not work on the subject that they worked on during the day or in their day job. Facebook chat and Facebook videos, two immensely popular features, were designed in single hackathons. Zuckerberg feels that in this way, a talented person's creativity can be best expressed. Since his college days, he himself was quite used to staying up till late in the morning, coding when it was quiet around. Hackathons though were all about DJs, music, food and drinks and of course, a lot of brainstorming.

The Fifteen Billion Dollar Company

Zuckerberg's dream of connecting the world had come true, at least in part. In the latter half of 2007, more than half of the Facebook members were outside of the United States, that too, without Facebook making any region-specific changes, not even of language. The cost of running the service throughout the world was increasing rapidly, and more money was needed. Also, the advertisements running on the site were specific to the US, so the company had to find an advertising partner for the international market. Peter Thiel, with his keen sense of timing, thought it was time that the company raised more money, something that Zuckerberg thanked him for later.

At that time, archrivals Microsoft and Google were battling for Internet dominance. For both, acquiring Facebook was a great way to ensure the same. Both started aggressively pursuing Facebook. Google approached with an unprecedented offer—a buyout for just a little less than 15 billion dollars. Zuckerberg, not even the slightest bit interested, declined the offer. Microsoft offered him 15 billion dollars. Again, he was not enticed. After a series of negotiations with Microsoft, a historic deal was announced. Microsoft acquired a miniscule 1.6 per cent of Facebook for an investment of 240 million dollars and gave it a market valuation of 15 billion dollars. Along with this, Hong Kong business magnate Li Ka-shing invested 60 million dollars for 0.4 per cent of Facebook. This was an unprecedented evaluation of a private company and the figures seemed bizarre, considering that Facebook had no actual profits to show. The media gasped in disbelief. A few months later, Li Ka-shing invested 60 million more. Investors Samwer Brothers from Munich also invested 15 million dollars. Consequently, Facebook now had 375 million dollars, enough to take it through the great financial depression that the world saw a year later.

RIP Facebook?

In November 2007, Facebook courted an outcry that threatened to damage not just the company's image but that of its founder's too. It was at a time when many people were shopping for the festive season. Suddenly, Facebook users started getting alerts in their News Feed about their friends' purchases. Since many of these were Christmas gifts, the surprises for friends and family were ruined. All of a sudden, people felt vulnerable. Their personal information, like the discounted item they bought, was being openly displayed. Their purchases of things, like film tickets, furniture and jewellery, were being broadcast to their friends. This was a potential disaster.

A few days ago, on 6 November of that year, Zuckerberg had made a presentation to the advertisers about the new form of advertising Facebook was launching. He had been against advertisements all along because he felt that most of the ads on the Internet or on TV were irrelevant to the user and many were totally absurd and irrelevant. He had a hatred of pop-up ads as well. Now, he had come up with the idea of 'social ads', a unique feature wherein any company could create a Facebook page for free and could advertise its products there. Members who joined the page would be called 'fans' instead of 'friends'. That fit into the Facebook culture, as it was not in-your-face advertising and was targeted only at potential customers.

The troublesome part was that, along with this, Facebook also launched a hastily designed feature called Beacon. The service had flaws and the design was not user-friendly. Beacon was an alert service that allowed 44 partner websites to send data to Facebook. Activities on these websites would also be reflected on the users' friends' News Feeds, even when a person was not logged on to the site. Facebook's purpose was to facilitate targeted advertising. It did not mean to transmit the information without consent, but this hastily designed service showed a very inconspicuous opt-out drop down and disappeared so quickly that most of the users did not even notice it.

Zuckerberg faced criticism from all quarters at this time. He had become one of the youngest billionaires ever and there were allegations that he had gotten so arrogant that he cared only about power and money and did not care about the users. Massive protests gained momentum. The public-policy advocacy group MoveOn.org led these protests. It held that Facebook was invading people's privacy and created a protest group that was quickly joined by around 68,000 users. Some other protest groups filed lawsuits.

The *Fortune* magazine wrote an obituary to Facebook with the title 'RIP Facebook'. It predicted the end of Facebook and went so far as to say, 'It could have all been avoided with a smart adult running things. Facebook has no old hands in its corner, no advisers to tell the kids how to behave. Netscape had its Jim Barksdale, Google (GOOG) its Eric Schmidt. This company has no one babysitting it. And watching it now is like watching an unattended child play with a pack of matches in a wooden house.'

The article further went on to add, 'In the space of a

month, it's gone from media darling to devil. The most interesting thing about Facebook right now is who will replace it.'[17] After the Microsoft evaluation, the company had been given the term 'the newest Internet darling' by the Wall Street Journal. The media was so obsessed with a 'kid' CEO that they failed to see that the problem was not with Zuckerberg's intentions but with the product design. The user control option appeared so briefly that it wasn't even noticeable. Zuckerberg made the mistake of not responding quickly to the situation. It was only on 29 November that a better system was put into place. A user could fully opt in, or no message would be sent without the user's consent. A week after this, Zuckerberg wrote a blog post in which he stated, 'We simply did a bad job with this release, and I apologize for it.'[18]

On Facebook's part, they were thinking that people might get used to Beacon the way they had accepted News Feed. Chamath Palihapitiya, Facebook's vice president for growth and internationalization told *The New York Times*, 'Whenever we innovate and create great new experiences and new features, if they are not well understood at the outset, one thing we need to do is give people an opportunity to interact with them... After a while, they fall in love with them.'[19]

It took them some time to realize that it was a real error on their part, but to apologize publicly and to acknowledge one's complacence shows a level of honesty. It also shows Zuckerberg as a person who takes ownership of his own as well as his team's mistakes. Facebook finally shut down Beacon in 2009. Yet, it had paved the way for a feature called Facebook Connect that was launched in 2008.

Handshakes and Goodbyes

In March 2008, Zuckerberg hired the 'Internet superstar' Sheryl Sandburg as the new chief operating officer of Facebook, but not without talking to her for more than fifty hours over a period of many days. Since then, her expertise has helped manage the company and its growth in a more systematic way, including monetization of the site. Soon after recruiting Sandberg, Zuckerberg left for a world trip and for a month, travelled to many places, including Istanbul, Japan and India. In India, he went for a spiritual visit to Kainchi Dham Ashram in Uttarakhand. In the days preceding this visit, he had been through a lot of stress and he made a trip to this temple on the suggestion of Steve Jobs, who had been inspired by this place.

With Sandberg working on streamlining things, Zuckerberg had found his correct number two. Soon after this, his original buddies moved on. Adam D'Angelo quit to start the website Quora and Dustin Moskovitz, the previously indispensable chum, left to begin working on his own software company called Asana. The friends left on cordial terms, knowing each other's personality too well to judge how long they could be work partners without losing the relationship of being friends. Chris Hughes, however, thinks Mark can be stiff where work is concerned, so he thought it was better to be just friends with him.

Upwards Is the Only Direction

The growth of Facebook continued in an unprecedented manner. In the middle of 2010, Facebook had around 500 million active users and by fall 2012, the number rose to one billion. In 2017, the number was over two billion. Zuckerberg added a lot of new features to the service including the 'like' button, live streaming and many more. Facebook gradually became a tool for growing business, for staying connected with family and for generating public opinion as well. The way this social network started having an impact, it had become an important part of the human ecosystem.

Recognition was bound to come to this young man whose focus and vision had built a revolutionary medium of communication. In 2010, he was ranked number one among the '100 most influential people of the information age' by *Vanity Fair* magazine. In the same year, he was chosen among the 50 most influential figures by *New Statesman*. But, perhaps, the most striking was this — Mark Zuckerberg was named the person of the year by *Time* magazine. This is what their headline read: 'For connecting more than half a billion people and mapping the social relations among them, for creating a new system of exchanging information and for changing how we live our lives, Mark Elliot Zuckerberg is TIME's 2010 Person of the Year.'[20]

At that time, it was a bit surprising that 70 per cent of Facebook's users were outside the United States. This fact brings to the fore an important aspect of Mark's personality. He could understand the human psyche, especially the domain of human communication, in a way that was not defined by the narrow constraints of culture or nationality. As *Time* aptly pointed out, at that time, if Facebook would be a country, it would be the third largest in terms of population. Mark had reached this destination because he kept the focus on his vision and was not tempted by fabulously extravagant offers of becoming rich. Yet, money does follow those who follow their vision. In 2018, Zuckerberg was the fifth richest man in the world with a net worth of over 70 billion dollars.

Tackling the Competition, Zuckerberg Style

Facebook is unique in this world of extensive Internet usage, including as much on mobile phones as on personal computers. There have been other social networking sites before it and there still are services that deal in some kind of social communication. Facebook has a place of its own because, right from the beginning, Zuckerberg designed it in a way that people used their real identities on Facebook. What makes it so different is that people sign up with their real names, instead of fancy or vague pseudonyms. Yet, Zuckerberg was never complacent about competition. Early on, Facebook had overtaken MySpace which ruled the Internet while Facebook was still growing.

This was mostly because of his keen eye for what is desirable in social interaction. He was also clear about keeping Facebook different from LinkedIn, as the latter was primarily about professionals uploading their resumes, though LinkedIn had launched a year before Facebook and people signed up with their real identities on this site too. Zuckerberg had initially thought about incorporating a resume or job search type of feature into Facebook. It was a smart move not to do so.

As Facebook's usage shot up at an unbelievable rate, Zuckerberg didn't lose sight of potential competition that could cut into its user base. Facebook has acquired more than 70 other companies, big and small. A lot of these have been small startups that had come up with products that could merge well with Facebook. More importantly, Mark Zuckerberg remains a perennial entrepreneur with a perpetual taste for entrepreneurship. He understands where the most creative things happen and has a liking for the creative, entrepreneurial mindset which is best found at startups. In a 2010 interview to *Business Insider,* he explained this, 'We have not once bought a company for the company. We buy companies to get excellent people... You come to Facebook because it is the best place where you learn how to build things.'[21] Thus, the acquisitions were primarily to get talented people to Facebook.

However, there were exceptions to this in two of the most talked-about acquisitions. The first one was Facebook buying Instagram for an inflated sum of one billion dollars in April 2012. The photo-sharing application Instagram had around 50 million users but practically no revenue. It was a smart acquisition because photo-sharing is one of the most popular activities on Facebook too. Instagram remained a standalone application and was not integrated into Facebook's features. Another major buyout that Facebook made was of the mobile messaging service WhatsApp in February 2014. Zuckerberg paid a whopping 19 billion dollars for this application that had more than 600 million users. People were quick to criticize Zuckerberg about this deal because WhatsApp had a revenue of just around 20 million dollars. The move, however, was very clever. WhatsApp had a growth rate that would have outdone Facebook easily—it was adding one million users every day at the time when Facebook's entire user base was 1.2 billion. In short, WhatsApp could do whatever Facebook could, but in a more convenient way. Thus, this decision could work out great wonders for Facebook.

Yet, even Mark Zuckerberg was spurned, at least once. In 2013, Facebook offered 3 billion dollars to buy Snapchat, but Evan Spiegel, the CEO of Snapchat turned down the offer. It is widely believed that, post this, Facebook worked intensively on using Instagram to destroy Snapchat. There have been allegations that some popular features were copied from Snapchat and incorporated into Instagram. Snapchat has lost users and has been struggling. Whatever the inside story might be, Zuckerberg has managed to keep his business alive and thriving.

Furthermore, 18 May 2012 turned out to be a historic day not just for Facebook but also for the stock exchange, as Facebook announced its Initial Public Offering (IPO). The reaction was unparalleled. Facebook was valued at 104 billion dollars, which was the highest a technology company had ever achieved. Zuckerberg's dorm room project had achieved another milestone.

THE MAN AND THE WORLD: THE FILM

Hollywood has a penchant for making films on famous people, but for Zuckerberg, it came rather too soon, just six years after he had launched Facebook from his dorm room. Many people today have formed an idea of Mark Zuckerberg the person after watching the film *The Social Network*, directed by David Fincher. The fact that the film won three Academy Awards has somehow endowed it with a mistaken authenticity. Although the makers of the film are entitled to their creative liberty, the film presents a lot of incorrect information about Zuckerberg.

The film is based on Ben Mezrich's book *The Accidental Billionaires: The Founding of Facebook, A Tale of Sex, Money, Genius and Betrayal*, which the author had written after

Eduardo Saverin approached him and told him only his side of the story. The author never interviewed Zuckerberg. Even Saverin stopped interacting with the author after an out-of-court settlement with Facebook. The book's publisher, Doubleday did not claim that it was all facts, mentioning, 'The book isn't reportage. It's big juicy fun.' The character of Mark is portrayed as a stiff, socially-incapable, desperate guy looking for girls. In one of his interviews, Zuckerberg complained that the filmmakers ignored the fact that one could build things because one wanted to build things (the reference is to software), and not build to get girls or to get into some clubs. The film was released in 2010, and went on to win three Academy Awards. Zuckerberg had complained about factual errors in the film, but was gracious enough to take it in good spirit, even appearing on *Saturday Night Live* with Jesse Eisenberg, the actor who had played him on screen. People who have closely known Mark, don't think that the film presents the correct information.

The Contentious Privacy Issues

Mark Zuckerberg has had the guts to innovate and to

constantly experiment. The process has involved quite a few difficult patches, the most obvious of which is the outrage over user-privacy-related issues. The root of the problem is that Facebook is not just a technology company; it is all about people and about people's communication data. Zuckerberg got a taste of this quite early with the News Feed and Beacon. The iconic 'like' button faced flak when it shared user preferences with outside partners. In 2009, Facebook had to revise its terms of service when there were protests against the fact that user data was not deleted when someone quit the service. In 2010, Facebook had to revise its privacy control settings again. In 2011 and again in 2013, the company had to face criticism for exposing users' personal data to third party applications.

The site has also been under pressure to manage how much data third-party applications can harvest from Facebook users. The largest of these pressure situations for Zuckerberg has been the Cambridge Analytica controversy. It turned out to be a major political scandal as it was revealed that Cambridge Analytica, a political consulting organization, had tapped into the personal data of millions of Facebook users and had used it to influence the presidential elections in the USA. Mark took responsibility for the situation and wrote a post that detailed how a researcher created a personality quiz application on the Facebook platform and could get hold of the personal data of at least 87 million users and later shared or sold the data to Cambridge Analytica. He wrote, 'We have a responsibility to protect your data, and if we can't then we don't deserve to serve you. I've been working to understand exactly what happened and how to make sure this doesn't happen again.'[22]

Zuckerberg even ran full-page apologies for the fiasco in at least ten newspapers. In April 2018, Zuckerberg testified before the United States Congress where, for two days, he was grilled by the American lawmakers. Wearing a suit and a tie, that are definitely not his staple, Zuckerberg patiently took questions from politicians, many of whom apparently do not understand the way information technology works. His apology is as straightforward as can be: 'It was my mistake, and I'm sorry… I started Facebook, I run it, and I'm responsible for what happens here.'[23]

Mark has never been shy of apologizing for the company's mistakes. He faces incessant criticism, many times because of his 'dictatorial' control over the company, since he holds the majority of the voting rights. On his part, Zuckerberg has strived to maintain an open environment in the company. He has insisted that at Facebook, employees are free to express their ideas; the culture is of openness and Facebook aims to be an idealistic company.

Other Controversies

In 2013, Zuckerberg initiated a project known as Internet. org and defined its purpose as providing free Internet services to 5 billion people who were not connected to the Internet. He said that his aim was to bring in more jobs and to improve the lives of the people in developing countries by bringing the Internet to them. However, the project received criticism for violating net neutrality, because only selective services would be free while others, including those offered by Facebook rivals, will have to be paid for. Moreover, the list of free services was decided by Facebook itself.

The service, renamed Free Basics, was banned by the Telecom Regulatory Authority of India because it was found to be functioning on discriminatory practices.

In 2018, Zuckerberg had to face allegations about

the improper practices employed by the firm Definers Public Affairs which was responsible for the public relations of Facebook. It was alleged that Definers planted malicious stories about Facebook's competitors, including Google. These stories were allegedly made available to the media. The firm was also accused of maligning the image of philanthropist George Soros who had criticized Facebook earlier. Facebook admitted that it had asked the firm to investigate if George Soros had any financial motivation to speak against Facebook. Everyday challenges for the Facebook boss have become routine, as the small project has grown to be a technology behemoth.

Power in the Hands of the People

While responding to the Cambridge Analytica issue, Zuckerberg had mentioned that while creating this site, he had never visualized that someone could use this technology to do something wrong. His hope has been partially fruitful with the way Facebook has helped fight against injustice and oppression. There is a profound impact that his creation has had on the world. It is well-known how the oppressive military,

FARC, in Columbia was defeated by protests that not only started on Facebook but were also organized and managed on this social network. Facebook's role in the Tunisian revolution demonstrates how this site could be a powerful tool of democracy. In times dominated by social media, anyone with a phone has the power to capture an image and to send a powerful message across the world. In 2017, Facebook played a crucial role in the relief efforts and in communicating important details after Hurricane Harvey, even as the US emergency contact number 911 remained out of reach.

The same power can become a weapon for spreading negative things like hatred, oppression, threats and misinformation. Zuckerberg has created an entity with enormous potential. The challenge before him is to try his best to make sure that the site is used for constructive purposes. This is a mammoth task, given the speed at which information circulates in this world of free information today.

The Individual: Personal Life

Besides running a company with more than 30,000 employees and facing constant criticism from different quarters, Mark Zuckerberg has a private life. His love life is a fairytale in its own right. In his Harvard commencement speech, Zuckerberg said that Priscilla is the most important person in his life, while she watched from the crowd and tried to hide the tears in her eyes that her husband's words had evoked. Priscilla was with Mark even before the launch of The Facebook. She was with him even when he was not famous or rich but was just a college dropout. The two had separated for a brief time when Zuckerberg had moved to Palo Alto. For a short while, he had another girlfriend, but he soon reunited with Chan when she came to California for her medical degree. Reportedly, she had set some conditions when they were together again; Mark would have to find time for at least a date every week and would have to spend at least a hundred minutes per week with her, which should be neither at his apartment, nor at Facebook.

Mark and Priscilla's wedding was quite a dramatic event as well. 19 May 2012 was the day that the couple had secretly planned as their wedding day. It happened to be the day after Facebook's IPO. The invited guests were told that it was a party to celebrate Priscilla's graduation. However, when the guests arrived at the couple's home, they came to know that the backyard of the house was, in fact, going to host the wedding.

Priscilla Chan, however, has an identity independent of being the wife of the Facebook CEO. She is a paediatrician and a philanthropist. Her influence on Mark has been most visible in his philanthropy, in promoting organ donation on Facebook and in pledging their money for the betterment of the health and education for children across the world. Chan has had a first-hand experience of the challenges faced by immigrants, coming from a family of Vietnamese-Chinese immigrants. She has been a teacher and has been a practising paediatrician, who has worked with children experiencing challenges, so she has an insight on the problems in healthcare and education.

The couple has two daughters, Maxima, who was born in 2015 and August, born in 2017. Zuckerberg sent a strong message to the world by taking a paternity leave of two months after the birth of his first child and another paternity leave in parts after the birth of his second child. The couple did face some sad times as Zuckerberg revealed in a Facebook post. Priscilla had suffered three miscarriages before having Maxima and the duo shared their pain with the world when they announced their first pregnancy.

The Philanthropist

In 2010, twenty-six-year-old Zuckerberg was on an Oprah Winfrey show when he made the announcement of donating a hundred million dollars to the Newark public schools of New Jersey, that had been facing issues for some time. Zuckerberg later revealed that he made the public announcement after the mayor urged him not to make an anonymous donation. An impressed Winfrey emphatically repeated the phrase 'a hundred million dollars'. But that was just the beginning of what Zuckerberg and his wife would do with their money. In December of that year, Zuckerberg joined The Giving Pledge along with Bill Gates and Warren Buffet. The Giving Pledge is an initiative to urge the super-rich of the world to donate most of their wealth, either during their lifetime or after their death.

In addition to that, when Chan and Zuckerberg welcomed their first child Maxima, they announced that they would donate 99 per cent of their Facebook shares over the course of their lives. They planned to direct this donation through The Chan Zuckerberg Initiative, which is working on research to bring medicine and technology together to make the world a better place to live in. The couple said that their inspiration for this was to help make the world healthier and safer for their children and all the children around the world. In 2013, Zuckerberg and Chan were among the 50 most generous Americans, a list compiled by *The Chronicle of Philanthropy*. By this time, they had made donations of over one billion dollars. Among their other donations is a twenty-five-billion-dollar donation to fight the Ebola virus.

Personal Goals

Zuckerberg is famous for setting a personal goal for himself every year. Sometimes the goals seem frivolous, but his purpose behind doing so is to constantly learn and improve. Some of these goals were for personal enhancement, such as the 2015 goal of reading a new book every two weeks, or writing a thank-you note every day, his goal for the year before that. His 2017 goal of visiting all the states of the US raised speculation about his political ambitions. However, for a man whose first love was coding, the passion keeps coming back. For 2012, he challenged himself to code every day and in 2016, he set the goal of coding an artificial intelligence assistant. For 2018, though, his goals were seriously intertwined with work. For that year, he set the goal of 'fixing' his site to tackle the problems that it was facing. Zuckerberg has to travel a lot, but he makes sure he spends time with his family and he exercises at least three days a week. He keeps his mind free of trivial matters by wearing similar clothes every day, a secret that he revealed a few years after everybody had been commenting on his uniform of grey t-shirts and jeans.

Mark Zuckerberg is Facebook's lowest-paid employee, with a salary of one dollar per annum. However, he is worth more than 77 billion dollars, based on his stock holdings in Facebook. As of 2018, his real estate wealth was around 175 million dollars, including a hundred-million-dollar piece of land in Hawaii.

The Incredible Journey

From a modest dormitory room to the heart of Silicon Valley, Mark Zuckerberg's journey has been incredible.

There were challenges at every step, but he never let any of the problems deter him from achieving what he wanted. He had a vision and he never let anything come in its way. There were hurdles, there were temptations, there was criticism, but none of these could prevent him from keeping his sight fixed on his goal. His inspirational self-belief is pleasantly mingled with a childlike acceptance of his mistakes, and the courage to apologize for those mistakes because, as he thinks, without the freedom to make mistakes, one cannot be successful. Zuckerberg's entrepreneurial journey also includes giving back to society. His influence will live not only through his charity, and through the communication revolution that he enacted, but also as a lesson in following one's passion to achieve success and the willingness to work hard, really hard, for it.

REFERENCES

1. https://news.harvard.edu/gazette/story/2017/05/mark-zuckerbergs-speech-as-written-for-harvards-class-of-2017/
2. http://nymag.com/news/features/zuckerberg-family-2012-5/index1.html
3. https://www.instagram.com/p/BRbd5S7DS1N/?hl=en
4. https://www.newyorker.com/magazine/2010/09/20/the-face-of-facebook
5. http://content.time.com/time/specials/packages/article/0,28804,2036683_2037183_2037185,00.html
6. https://www.scribd.com/document/538696/mark-zuckerbergs-harvard-application
7. https://news.slashdot.org/story/03/04/21/110236/machine-learning-and-mp3s
8. https://www.cnbc.com/2017/05/31/mark-zuckerberg-the-idea-of-a-single-eureka-moment-is-a-lie.html
9. https://www.thecrimson.com/article/2003/12/11/put-online-a-happy-face-after/
10. Ibid.
11. https://www.thecrimson.com/article/2004/5/28/online-facebooks-duel-over-tangled-web/?page=single

12. Kirkpatrick, David, *The Facebook Effect: The Real Inside Story of Mark Zuckerberg and the World's Fastest Growing Company*, RHUK, 2011

13. https://web.archive.org/web/20050117052114/ http://www.chronicle.duke.edu/vnews/display.v/ ART/2004/04/14/407d22986b0d0?in_archive=1%2F

14. Kirkpatrick, David, *The Facebook Effect: The Real Inside Story of Mark Zuckerberg and the World's Fastest Growing Company*, RHUK, 2011

15. Kirkpatrick, David, *The Facebook Effect: The Real Inside Story of Mark Zuckerberg and the World's Fastest Growing Company*, RHUK, 2011

16. https://www.youtube.com/watch?v=5WiDIhIkPoM

17. http://fortune.com/2007/12/04/rip-facebook/

18. https://techcrunch.com/2007/12/05/zuckerberg-saves-face-apologies-for-beacon/

19. 17https://www.nytimes.com/2007/11/30/technology/30face.html

20. http://content.time.com/time/specials/packages/article/0,28804, 2036683_2037183_2037185,00.htm

20. www.youtube.com/watch?v=OlBDyItD0Ak

22. https://www.facebook.com/story.php?story_fbid=10104 712037900071&id=4

23. https://www.washingtonpost.com/video/politics/zuckerberg-i-started-facebook-i-run-it-and-im-responsible-for-what-happens-here/2018/04/10/24c71e64-3cf2-11e8-955b-7d2e19b79966_video.html?utm_term=.8b503774215e

Also in *The Making of the Greatest* Series

JEFF BEZOS

by Sangeeta Pandey

This book looks at some of the defining moments and key incidents from the life of Jeffrey Preston Bezos, the world's first centibillionaire, and the journey he undertook to make Amazon the most valued company in the world.

Amazon's brilliant, visionary founder, Jeff Bezos, continues to be the driving force behind the company's astounding and continued success. From being on the verge of bankruptcy during the 1990s, Amazon is now a household name. Even after achieving so much, Jeff's passion for innovation has only increased. His new pet project — Blue Origin — aims to make space travel affordable in order to colonize other planets. Clearly, Jeff has taken the meaning of 'long-term vision' to another level.

A role model to entrepreneurs across the world, this is a man who can predict tomorrow better than anyone else.

BILL GATES

by Ajay Sethi

Encyclopaedia Britannica describes Bill Gates (born William Henry Gates III) as an 'American computer programmer, businessman and philanthropist' — and rightly so. However, the man and his achievements are so vast that even a big, fat encyclopaedia would not be enough to document his entire life.

In his teenage years, Gates acquired the reputation of being quite a hacker. At thirteen, he hacked his school computer and got himself into a class 'with a disproportionate number of interesting girls'. Then, at fifteen, he hacked the computer of a big corporation. He has even been arrested. His life took a dramatic turn in 1975 when he decided to drop out of Harvard. Soon after, he and Paul Allen co-founded Microsoft Corporation out of a garage in Albuquerque, New Mexico. By the end of the 1980s, Microsoft had become the largest software company in the world. A billionaire since 1986, Gates is currently the second richest man in the world, behind Amazon's Jeff Bezos.

This book is about a man who changed not only the way people live and work every day but also redefined the meaning of 'giving back to society' by pledging most of his wealth to charity.

JACK MA

by Abha Sharma

This is the incredible story of Jack Ma, who was branded as a failure but chose not to give up.

Jack Ma (born Ma Yun) studied at an ordinary institution in China and failed multiple times as a student, and yet he held on to self-belief and created the Alibaba Group, the largest e-commerce company in the world. He was rejected for more than thirty jobs, including that of a waiter, but a few years down the line, he was providing employment to millions of people. He first experienced the Internet at age thirty, but such was his business acumen that he built a company that wouldn't exist without the Internet. He learned English by talking to tourists, but he is one of the most admired public speakers in the language.

He says, 'If Jack Ma and his team can be successful, eighty per cent of the people [...] can be successful.' How did Jack Ma achieve all of this in the face of constant adversity?

Get an insight into the gruelling yet amazing work culture that he built at Alibaba. Jack Ma's story has that magical capability of invoking the best in people, to inspire them to persevere and keep moving ahead, and to make them think beyond self-interest.